Two Guns to Apache Wells

Rancher's daughter Rebecca Donnell was sentenced to death after recognizing one of the men who robbed the stage she was travelling on. Her father knew only that she had vanished off the face of the earth, so he hired the only two men he felt could possibly find her – or her body . . . Shane Preston and Jonah Jones.

The two gunfighters rode into the wilderness with no guarantees of success, but once they took a man's money they never quit a job until it was complete. First they found the missing stagecoach, or what was left of it. Then they found three shallow graves. . . .

Their quest should have ended there. But the lean gunfighter and his crusty old companion knew they wouldn't rest until they settled with the killers themselves, the so-called Long Knife Gang.

Meanwhile, there was a pack of renegades on their trail, determined to capture and torture them for shooting their chief's kill-crazy son.

There was no turning back for Shane and Jonah. They were caught smack in the middle of two bands of killers who were both set on taking their scalps!

Two Guns to Apache Wells

Cole Shelton

A Black Horse Western

ROBERT HALE

First published by Cleveland Publishing Co. Pty Ltd,
New South Wales, Australia
First published in 1967

© 2019 by Piccadilly Publishing

This edition © The Crowood Press, 2020

ISBN 978-0-7198-3118-8

The Crowood Press
The Stable Block
Crowood Lane
Ramsbury
Marlborough
Wiltshire SN8 2HR

www.bhwesterns.com

Robert Hale is an imprint
of The Crowood Press

ONE

STAGE RIDE TO HELL

The westbound stagecoach skidded to a shuddering halt, its horses plunging at the line of boulders rolled right across the trail. Dust billowed into the moonlit void and, perched precariously on his driver's seat, old Luke Stearnes felt the stagecoach rock to a creaking standstill beneath him. From inside the stage came sharp curses from one of the soldiers, while his female passenger let out a stifled scream. And swiftly, like the five fingers of an evil hand, the masked riders closed in.

Luke Stearnes didn't move.

5

He knew that the long rifle resting by his boot was but a moment away from his grasp, but the old-timer wasn't planning to play the hero. Instead, he watched white-faced as the outlaw band swooped. One of them reined in beside the stack of boulders they'd rolled across the trail to force the stage to its frantic halt. Two others sat saddle with guns poised, while the remaining riders approached the stagecoach door, and when the tallest outlaw glanced up at Stearnes, the old driver glimpsed the cold, gray eyes slitted just above the bandanna mask.

'All right!' came the muffled voice. 'Open that door and climb down with your paws high!'

'Driver!' The tone was high-pitched, and the rider by the boulders leveled his six-gun at Stearnes. 'I reckon you'll have a gun up there. Toss it down!'

Stearnes bent down. Gnarled fingers grasped the rifle barrel and lifted the Winchester high. The outlaws watched him as he dropped it into the dust and began to clamber down himself. His boots found the powdery trail dust and he stood beside the stage as the door creaked wide.

'Well, now!' mocked the tall outlaw. 'A soldier-boy! Come on out, soldier-boy!'

Corporal Martin jumped down and stood awkwardly next to Luke Stearnes. The tall outlaw sniggered beneath his mask as Martin slowly raised his gloved hands high and muttered a harsh curse. Another shadow fell from the stage door, bringing a second jibe from the tall, lean outlaw. Trooper de Dino stepped down, swaying a little uncertainly. He was red-faced, his eyes puffed, and the half-empty bottle of whisky which had been his constant trail-companion since leaving the way-station now rolled on the stage floor.

'Come on, ma'am!' The lanky outlaw leaned forward in his saddle. 'Or do I have to climb in and fetch you out?'

Rebecca Donnell was trembling and her face was white with fear. Leaning out of the stage, she simply stared at the stark riders and their naked gun-muzzles. The moon framed her as she tentatively grasped the stage door and then slowly eased herself out. Stearnes glanced at her, suddenly looking back at the tall raider, whose eyes were now roving frankly over Rebecca's slender figure.

The outlaw continued to appraise her like a man sizing up a steer he was about to buy.

'Held up a few stages in my time, ma'am,' he said softly. 'Run across a number of women, too. But you sure are the prettiest filly I've come across to date.'

'Jeb!' The sharp, brittle voice belonged to the rider who'd been sitting his saddle alongside the tall man. 'Get on with it! You know why we're here!'

'Sure,' purred the rangy owlhoot, Jeb. He surveyed Luke Stearnes menacingly. 'Where's the payroll, driver?'

Stearnes swallowed and Jeb's gun swiveled around to point at his belly.

'What payroll?' Stearnes finally found his voice.

For a long moment, Jeb merely stared at the stage driver. Then he levered his frame out of the saddle and stood in front of Stearnes. He was a lean, thin rake of a man silhouetted against the drenching moonlight, and his masked face was a dark menace. Stearnes held his breath and a split second later, the outlaw's gun butt smashed into his face. The stage driver cried out in agony and reeled back against the stagecoach. He clawed at the wheel, his head spinning, warm, sticky blood gushing from a cruel groove below his left eye. He flopped to the ground and Corporal Martin's strong hands hauled him to his feet. Panting, Stearnes stood shaking as the tall outlaw toyed with his gun.

'Where's the payroll, driver?' the outlaw repeated slowly and deliberately.

'The Fort Sanderson payroll?' It was Martin, standing stiffly to attention and taking over from Stearnes.

They could see the outline of the outlaw's grin beneath the fabric of the red bandanna.

'Nice to see a soldier-boy cooperating,' the raider

smirked. 'Sorta revives my faith in the military.'

'It's government money,' Corporal Martin stated bluntly. He was red-faced and angry and his gray eyes twitched. 'Steal it, and the army will never let up in hunting you down.'

'Hear that, boys?' Jeb mocked. 'We'll be in trouble if we steal the soldier-boy's money!'

Several of them guffawed but the beefy rider with the brittle voice spurred his horse right up to the stage. The big bay he rode pawed the dust and the outlaw's eyes were twin furnace-holes of hot fury.

'For Pete's sake!' he snapped impatiently. 'Quit playing games and grab that payroll!'

'Sure, boss,' Jeb shrugged. He turned back to Corporal Martin. 'You know where the payroll is, soldier-boy. Climb inside and fetch it for us.'

The outlaw thumbed back the hammer of his Colt and the metallic click echoed out in the silence of the desert. The soldier stared at the cold gun muzzle and turned around. He shoved past Trooper de Dino and peered in at the darkness of the stage's interior. He looked at the wooden seats, the long, knotty planks upon which the passengers had bounced together as the stage-wheels bumped over the trail-ruts. His eyes dropped to the darker recesses beneath the seats. Mostly the bags and cases there belonged to Rebecca Donnell. A woman on her way to be married needs more baggage than most. Martin's gaze fell upon the tin box that he and de Dino were responsible for. The gray box holding the fort's payroll.

Sweat beaded his brow.

The army could hardly blame him in this instance, but Corporal Martin knew instinctively that the loss of the payroll would have a detrimental effect on his chances of promotion.

The army rarely bought excuses. Suddenly his eyes dropped to the army carbine, propped within arm's reach.

'Hurry up, damn you!' The outlaw with the brittle voice pointed his gun at Martin's back. 'Fetch it out!'

Corporal Martin clambered inside. His right hand groped for the payroll box and he hauled it across the floor. Holding the tin box, the soldier jumped out. With a heave, he tossed the payroll container into the dust, and like vultures, the outlaws swooped from their horses.

Yelling and laughing, the masked men grabbed at the box, passing it from one to the other. Tall Jeb finally threw it onto the ground again and leveled his gun at the padlock. There was a deafening roar, and the padlock snapped like a dry twig. Eager, hungry hands forced the lid open.

Furtively, Martin swung his body around, edging his hand back along the floor of the stagecoach.

Blindly, his fingers raked the darkness for the carbine. Flesh closed over steel. The soldier began to drag the gun across the wooden floor, and with a sharp flick, he whipped it out of the stage.

There was a wild cry of warning from an outlaw mouth. Corporal Martin swung his carbine to aim at the nearest renegade, but the beefy outlaw-boss already had his six-gun aimed. The blast was like a whipcrack and the slug burned point-blank into the soldier's chest. Martin was lifted against the stage and as he slithered downwards, he desperately tried to level his carbine. Then he sagged and this time Jeb's bullet slashed into his ribs. Corporal Martin pitched forward like a felled tree, but even as he hit the ground, his carbine exploded in a violent spasm. The bullet winged low and wide, hitting the flank of the outlaw leader's horse.

The big bay reared in pain and terror, its hoofs etched against the moon.

Hastily, the outlaw-boss stepped backward, but the hapless horses thudded against him as its hoofs stamped down like twin iron hammers. The outlaw croaked in anguish, crashing to the ground only inches from the pummeling hoofs.

Instantly, willing hands hauled him up, but when he'd fallen, his bandanna had been dislodged, and now it flopped down over his neck. The exposed face

11

was ashen and stubbled.

'By hell!' Luke Stearnes rasped as he stared unbelievingly at the face he'd seen many times in Boulder Bluff. 'You! You leading this bunch of bastards!'

The outlaw-boss blasted him, drowning out any further words, ripping a hole through the old stage-driver's heart. Luke Stearnes plunged down without a murmur, and Rebecca screamed frantically as he lay motionless and bloodied at her feet.

The thick-set outlaw-boss pulled the bandanna back over his face, but he knew that the damage had already been done. Rebecca Donnell was staring incredulously at his masked face, her lips framing the name of the man whose integrity was unquestioned in Boulder Bluff. Even de Dino knew him, and now the little trooper held his breath.

'Jeb,' the outlaw leader said. 'Take the payroll back to the camp. I'll be riding out there later.'

He stalked past the wounded bay and selected another horse.

'What about these, boss?' the tall Jeb wanted to know, indicating the trooper and the weeping girl.

'Reckon you know the answer to that one, Jeb,' the man grunted. 'They've both recognized me, and that sure means they can't go riding back to town. In fact, they can't go riding back anywhere. Kill them, Jeb! I want no survivors, no one left alive to talk!'

'Sure,' Jeb smiled.

'In fact,' the boss said pensively. 'I want no trace of anything. No stage, no survivors, no clues. Get what I mean? Reckon there's someplace in this desert they can all be hidden permanently.'

'Leave it to me, boss.' Jeb pulled down his red bandanna. His face was bronzed, like an Indian's, and there was a hideous black scar running down from the corner of his left eye to the prominent bridge of his nose. 'See you in a couple of days.'

The leader wheeled his mount around and headed east for the long, twisted ridge that sliced the moonlit sky. The outfit watched his dust recede.

'Riding back to where he's respectable!' Jeb quipped to the petrified girl. 'Bet you never guessed he's Long Knife, leader of this outfit, huh? They tell me he's a pillar of the community back in Boulder Bluff!'

Hands pulled bandannas down. Faces were bared in the night. The dark, hard faces of the notorious Long Knife outfit! Rebecca had ceased to weep. Sheer terror dried up her tears and froze the pleas in her throat. Beside her, Trooper de Dino was whimpering like a whipped dog and suddenly the gun blast sounded. The soldier pitched forward, sprawling on his face. Blood oozed out over the dust and Rebecca turned her head away, her hands clinging to the side of the stagecoach. Any moment now she expected the bullet which would snuff out her life, slice like a hot knife into her back. She found herself whispering the name of the man she'd been on her way to marry. She heard the hammer of the gun being edged back. She shut her eyes tight as hard metal jabbed into the flesh of her neck.

'Know something, ma'am?'

It was Jeb's voice, strangely hollow now.

Rebecca shivered.

She was conscious that the shadows were moving even closer, hemming her in around the stage. She could hear their heavy breathing and the low snicker moments before Jeb's hand came to rest on her shoulder.

'Know something, ma'am?' Jeb repeated. 'Seems a damn shame to kill a pretty woman like you. One helluva waste, that's what I say.'

Jeb's hand swiveled her around and now she faced him. She shuddered.

Very slowly, Jeb replaced the gun in its holster. 'Mind, ma'am,' the tall outlaw said solemnly, 'can't say as I blame the boss. He wouldn't want anyone turnin' up in town and spillin' out the truth. Of course, I could keep you alive but make sure you couldn't ever go back and spill what you know. How about that?'

14

'Please!' Rebecca forced out a pathetic whisper.

'And back at our camp, you sure won't be talking to no one, no one that is except us.'

Rebecca Donnell closed her eyes once more. Her fate had just been spelled out for her, and there was nothing she could do about it. She could scream, plead, even try to run, but it would be all to no avail. She was in their hands, a captive at their mercy. If they so desired, they could murder her, just like they'd murdered all the other passengers on this doomed stage.

But right now they had something other than killing on their minds.

Jeb let his big hand slip from her shoulder to her silken black hair, and Rebecca held her breath as he stroked it. Then his hand roved to the swell of her young breasts and his fingers lingered on the top button of her dress.

'Well now, boys,' Jeb grinned as their eyes burned at their prisoner. 'Reckon we owe it to ourselves to take a closer look-see at our prize.'

Petrified, frozen by the kind of terrible fear only a woman can know, Rebecca stood there like a statue as Jeb's greedy fingers worked feverishly at her buttons.

The wilderness which had been a heated crucible by day was now a cold sea of dust, lifeless trees and marbled boulders. The hundreds of flies that had buzzed and bitten the possemen since sun-up had been replaced by hordes of droning mosquitoes. It was sundown, and the dying veins of purple stretched across the western void and painted the lonely old buttes that stood like silent sentinels in this ancient land. A chill wind had whipped in from the north and now it whispered around the tired riders as they reined in beneath an awesome granite rim. No one had actually suggested making camp, but every man knew that it was here that they'd spend the night. Their horses were weary, Kenning's big chestnut was nearly lame and the men themselves were fit to drop.

Only old Ridge Donnell stayed in the saddle as one by one the possemen eased their tired frames to the sand. It had not been their fault that this search had been a fruitless one. For three days now these men had stayed away from the comforts of home to look for the lost stage, the westbound which had never reached Sonora. And yet they'd found no trace. They'd stopped by the way-station, learnt that the stage had actually left there to strike out for the mesa, but from then on there was no trace.

'The men are all in, Ridge,' Pete Kenning told him quietly. The owner of the ranch adjoining Donnell's was standing beside him in the fading light. 'This is where we'll be stopping.'

Rebecca Donnell's father still sat his saddle. He was a wan shadow against the backdrop of dying day. The other members of the posse were attending to their horses while Sheriff Buchan was gathering wood for the campfire.

'Yeah,' Donnell nodded. His gnarled old hands fumbled for his tobacco-sack.

'We've done all we can, Ridge.' There was the weariness of defeat in Pete Kenning's voice. 'I reckon that's all a man can ask for.'

'Uh huh, Pete,' Ridge Donnell murmured. 'And I sure am grateful.'

Donnell let his eyes rove over the men. These possemen, all sworn in as deputies, had given their time freely and without asking for reward. It was at a time like this that a man's real friends stood up to be counted. There was Pete Kenning, dust-plastered, gray haired, a somber man who'd given his services willingly, spending time away from his ranch and business interests. Standing beside the mounting pile of dead wood for the fire was Ed Buchan, the town sheriff, and close to him was Al Witting, part-owner of the flourishing Lodestone Silver Mine. Witting was a tall man, young, ambitious, and Donnell had been more than surprised when he'd volunteered to join this posse. Unsaddling his gray was Bern O'Neill, one of Pete Kenning's range-riders. O'Neill was a former

17

army scout, but even his talents had proved inadequate in this search. Few words were being exchanged right now. They were men who'd failed and they had to ride home beaten.

Donnell said, 'We've had three hard days on the trail.'

'And nights,' Kenning reminded him. 'Hell, Ridge! It's got me beat. How can a damn stage just vanish? Old Stearnes was the driver, and he knows the desert trails like the back of his hand.'

'A stage can't just vanish.' Ridge Donnell reflected bitterly on the fact that his daughter, on her way to get married had disappeared, too. Donnell lit his cigarette and the red glow lit up a face that had aged a decade, lined with lines of grief.

Very slowly, Donnell eased himself out of the saddle. Pete Kenning held his horse for him, and then placed an arm around the rancher's shoulders.

'On her way to get her wedding dress fitted.' Donnell was torturing himself again. 'My wife and I were to follow in a week's time.'

'Try to figure out what could have happened, Ridge.' Kenning forced himself to sound optimistic. 'Maybe old Stearnes took sick and wandered off-trail.'

Donnell shook his head. 'Pete, you know what this desert holds. Badlanders, renegade Indians! Both of us know what musta happened.'

'Ridge,' Kenning said quietly. 'Come and join the boys around the fire.'

The meal was a subdued affair. The weary, red-eyed men drank hot coffee and ate salted meat in near-silence. Beyond the flickering campfire coyotes padded around the rocks and howled under the big rim like a pack of wolves. Cigarettes were lit. O'Neill uncorked a bottle of whisky. The possemen tried to persuade Donnell to have a drink, but he politely declined. Loneliness engulfed him. These men were his friends, but suddenly, feeling the utter hopeless-ness of the situation, he sank into the depths of despair. He stood up and walked out into the night.

Beyond the camp, the darkness enclosed him in its cold black hand.

He found a flat boulder and sat down. He was thinking of his daughter and the last time he'd seen her. It was at the stage-depot in Boulder Bluff, and she'd left him, flushed and excited, a girl on her way to be a bride, to be fulfilled. Now, God alone knew where she was.

'Ridge.'

It was Ed Buchan, Boulder Bluff's paunchy, flabby-faced little lawman, decidedly overweight with a belly that flopped over his belt. The top of his head reached only to Donnell's shoulder, but what he lacked in stature he made up for in raw courage.

Almost single-handed, he'd made the streets of Boulder Bluff safe for decent citizens to walk down, even at night. But this time, even Buchan had to admit he was beaten.

'Maybe – maybe if we'd gotten the news earlier,' Sheriff Ed Buchan said, 'we coulda got a lead.'

Donnell dismissed the lawman's statement. 'The Sonora stage depot wired you when the stage was ten hours late. Reckon that was reasonable, Ed. For all they knew in Sonora, the stage might have broken an axle and was just running late. And anyhow, when you did get the news, it didn't take over-long to gather together a posse of deputies. I guess we did our best, Ed. We did all we could.'

Ed Buchan fidgeted. 'Come back and join us at the fire, Ridge.'

'Not right now, Ed. I came out here so I could think.'

'It won't do you no good,' the sheriff said. 'Hell, Ridge. Me and the boys can see what this is doing to you '

'I'm thinking just how I'll write some letters, Ed,' the rancher explained. 'Workin' 'em out in my mind.'

'Letters, huh?'

'One's to Stobie.'

'Rebecca's intended?' Ed Buchan frowned darkly

20

and began to pick his words with care. 'Mind you, Ridge, can't say as I was exactly impressed with him.'

There was a long silence.

Buchan drew on his cigarette in the darkness, then went on. 'Kinda recall the time Rebecca brought him back to Boulder Bluff for a week. Met him in church, He – ah – struck me as sorta dandified.' The lawman cleared his throat. 'Wouldn't say that to anyone else, mind, but I figure you and me know each other well enough for me to come right out with it.'

Ridge Donnell said nothing. He wasn't going to bother defending Oliver Stobie. In actual fact, like Buchan, he'd never taken to the young man Rebecca had met on one of her frequent trips to visit her cousin in Sonora, but Stobie was his daughter's choice, and maybe that's all that really mattered.

'By now, of course,' Donnell said, 'Stobie'll know something's wrong. So I reckon I'll be writing to him just to let him know how we searched for the stage.'

'Know somethin', Ridge?' Sheriff Ed Buchan pursued the subject of Oliver Stobie. 'If I'd been Rebecca's man, I'd have wired Boulder Bluff myself if she was even two hours late. As it was, the stage depot wired. Not a damn word from the man she was headin' west to marry.'

'Maybe there was a reason,' Donnell said indifferently. 'Could be he rode out on the trail looking for

21

the stage himself.'

'Could be,' Buchan said cynically, and then, 'You mentioned more letters, Ridge.'

'Uh huh,' Donnell murmured. 'Second one'll cost me plenty, but I figure Rebecca's worth it.'

'Huh?' The lawman sounded mystified.

'Letter's kinda personal, Ed.'

Buchan shrugged, but taking the hint, didn't press the point. The two men smoked alone, each deep in thought. Ed Buchan had dismissed this second letter from his mind and he was thinking about the comforts of home, of his buxom, sensuous wife. On the other hand, Ridge Donnell was recalling a conversation he'd once had with Josh Connor, a rancher from Kansas. Connor's spread had been plagued by the Ringo outfit, a ruthless rustling gang that almost stripped his spread. Lawmen and vigilantes failed. Posses were unable to run down the bunch. But one day Connor hired two men, and these riders came into his valley and cracked down on the rustlers. The bunch was destroyed and the Ringo brothers who led, finally hanged. However, Josh Connor had pointed out, these two gunfighters were no ordinary men. They weren't exactly beloved by law officers. They didn't always fight by the rulebook, and that was one reason why he wasn't going to mention them to Sheriff Ed Buchan. They were men who hired out their guns for cash, and Josh Connor had paid them plenty. Even now, Donnell knew that their fees would be equal to one man's paydirt for a year, but like he'd said, Rebecca was worth it. Of course, the gunhawks mightn't be interested in the chore, but Donnell reckoned they were his only chance of finding Rebecca. This posse had failed, through no fault of any man who'd ridden on it, and Donnell figured there was no one around Boulder Bluff who was capable of doing any better.

'Reckon I'll be getting back to the fire,' the lawman said, and waddled away, leaving Ridge Donnell alone with his thoughts.

Back on his desk was a slip of paper Connor had given him in case he ever needed it. Written on this slip was the forwarding address of the two men he'd once hired. Donnell stubbed his cigarette on the boulder.

He knew what he had to do, and his only regret was that he hadn't done it earlier, but the posse had called out at his ranch almost immediately after Buchan received that wire, and at the time all Donnell had been interested in was joining them. Besides, he recalled the confidence of the possemen at the time. No stage could simply vanish! They'd bring it back sure enough! But now, the posse defeated, he had that letter to write. He didn't aim to tell anybody about his proposed invitation. The men Connor had told him about wouldn't want to ride in with the town knowing about their mission. That wasn't the way they liked to do things. Donnell glanced back at the fire. Now he could rejoin his friends. His mind was made up. The moment he got back to his spread, he was going to write a letter to Shane Preston and Jonah Jones.

TWO

TRAIL TO MYSTERY

They came down from the northern ranges with the red dust still clinging to the sweat of their horses and the hot noon sun blasting their leathery faces. They came across the plains where the yellowing grass whispered against their stirrups and where the last great herds of shaggy buffalo lumbered away at their approach. And by early afternoon they headed past the towering, contorted pinnacle of pumice that cast its needle shadow over the valley.

Plunging down from the rim, the riders dropped to the valley floor, only stopping for their weary horses to drink from the aspen-lined creek, and then turning down-trail towards the patchwork quilt of ranches and sodbuster spreads. To the west, the sleepy buildings of Boulder Bluff rested in the heat haze, but the riders weren't interested in visiting town. Their destination was the biggest ranch in the valley.

It was some valley, wide and long, crisscrossed by a hundred fences. Tiny ten-acre nester farms were sandwiched between huge rolling spreads. A horse-ranch spanned two ridges. Three cattle ranches dominated the southern side of the trail and a score of miners' shacks clung to the banks of the creek.

Finally the taller and younger of the two riders reined in.

'I reckon, Jonah,' Shane Preston said, leaning forward in the saddle, 'that this here's about the end of the trail.'

Craggy old Jonah Jones breathed a sigh of relief as he read the sign his companion had spotted first. It was a large square board hanging over a white gate, and it proclaimed that the Lazy-D belonged to Ridge Donnell and that trespassers would be shot.

'Well,' the older gunfighter grinned, 'I guess we ain't trespassers, Shane. We was invited.'

'We sure was,' Shane said. The envelope containing Donnell's urgent letter still protruded from his vest pocket like a white 'kerchief against the stark black of his shirt. 'Let's ride in and introduce ourselves to this Mr Donnell.'

They rode up to the gate, the tall man in black making a sharp contrast with his palomino mount, and the older, plumper Jonah urging his tiring mare to keep up. Shane reached the gate first and leaned over to unhook the latch. He kicked the gate wide and rode on through, then waited patiently for Jonah, who was having trouble persuading his plodding mare, Tessie, that right now wasn't the right time for a spell. Finally the oldster drew alongside Shane.

The two gunslingers let their eyes rove over the domain of the Lazy-D.

Vast grasslands stretched to the far wall of the valley and hundreds of steers grazed around the waterhole fed by a branch of the creek. Shane had never met the Lazy-D's owner but by the looks of this spread, Donnell could well afford the thousand dollars he'd offered in his letter.

It was, Shane reflected, the biggest amount of paydirt offered them since they'd started riding together. At the time of the letter's arrival, they'd been preparing to visit an old friend of Jonah's, but the trip had been postponed. Shane had been mildly surprised by the short, terse note they'd received, a letter obviously written by a man in deep distress and betraying a strange faith in two gunslingers he'd never met but whom he'd heard of through Josh Connor. A vacation with Jonah's friend would have been welcome, but Donnell's problem was more pressing. Besides, the rancher was offering a thousand dollar fee!

Shane headed across the grass as Jonah swung his boot at the gate. The entrance-gate shuddered shut, and moments later the two men were riding down the gentle slope. The trail dropped past the waterhole and steeped to a narrow ridge. The riders passed a cowboy who yelled a greeting from the shade of a cottonwood, and soon they were reining in on the crest. Below, a stately ranch house basked in the warm sun.

'Hell. . . !' Jonah Jones said reverently, his right hand stroking his shaggy white beard. 'Take a look-see at that!'

Shane whistled softly at the hand-carved columns and the Spanish windows, and his eyes moved slowly over the adobe brick and slate roof of the ranch house which showed in a flash Ridge Donnell's extravagance, power and money.

'So we take a look inside that castle,' Shane grinned.

Shane led the way. He was a lean streak of a man, raw-boned, rugged as the mountains he loved. He was a man who stood out in any crowd, not just because he dressed in black but because of his towering stature. You'd hardly call Shane Preston handsome, although more than one woman had wanted him, but there was something about him that compelled respect, even awe. Maybe it was the way his piercing eyes summed a man up. Maybe it was the way he carried the notched gun low-slung in its black holster.

The palomino, Snowfire, pawed the ground as Shane halted beside the front picket fence that divided the ranch house from the corrals.

Jonah looked at the neatly arranged rose-garden and the carefully tended shrubs which graced the front.

'You two hombres expected?'

The question came from a bow-legged cowpoke who'd ambled over to them from the outbuildings. He was flanked by a seedy-looking individual with an unlit cigarette drooping from his thick lips.

Shane surveyed them, his cold, aloof eyes moving briefly from one to the other. The bowlegged ranny looked uneasy as Shane's stare took him in. 'Take us to Donnell,' Shane said crisply. 'The name's Shane Preston.'

'Preston!' The bow-legged one planted his hands on his hips in a sudden display of bravado. 'You can't just walk in and throw orders around!'

'No?' Shane's voice was icy.

'Jake!' The seedy-looking cowboy nudged his companion.

'Huh?'

'Take a look.' He jerked his head at the notched black handle of Shane's six-gun nestling in its black leather holster. 'This ain't no saddlebum!'

Jake gulped, then said, 'Follow me, gents.'

Wordlessly, the two gunfighters followed the cowboy as he headed for the front door. It was a carved, Spanish-style door with an ornamental knocker. The cowpoke pushed open the door and strode inside with the two gunslingers following him down the dark hallway, their boots clattering on the polished tile floor. The ranch-hand hesitated at a side door, then rapped cautiously on it.

'Who is it?' The voice from inside was gruff.

'Coupla gents to see you, boss.'

The cowpoke stepped aside as Shane shoved the door wide. The tall gunhawk paced inside and Donnell rose hurriedly from his chair.

'Name's Shane Preston,' the gunslinger introduced himself. 'And this here's my pard.'

'Jonah Jones,' the white-haired gunhawk supplied.

Donnell glanced past Jonah to where the bow-legged cowhand stood gaping in the doorway.

'It's OK, Jake,' he said impatiently.

With a shrug, Jake closed the door.

Ridge Donnell extended a hand which Shane gripped firmly. He could feel the rancher trembling.

'Thank you, thank you for coming, gentlemen,' Donnell greeted them, gratitude breaking up his voice into a croak.

Gentlemen! Jonah grinned from ear to ear. It wasn't often they were referred to in this manner. The oldster straddled a chair, his wide eyes moving over the cedar furniture, the oil paintings and the shelves of books that graced Ridge Donnell's office.

'I'll fix you drinks,' Donnell said, walking to the door. He thrust it wide. 'Rona!' he called.

There was a rustle of skirts, and a few moments later, a dark-skinned girl presented herself. Shane afforded her a cursory glance, taking in the black braids of her hair and the flashing brown eyes which met his.

Rona smiled at the two guests.

'I want the best bottle of brandy in the place,' Donnell told her. 'And three glasses.'

Donnell resumed his seat as Rona glided back down the passage. It was then that his welcoming smile gave way to a troubled frown, and finally he lifted melancholy eyes to his two guests. Shane could see the depths of grief mirrored in the lines of his face, the desperation of a man grasping at straws.

'Let's get straight to the point, Mr Donnell,' Shane

31

said. He wasn't the kind of man to stand on ceremony. 'You sent us a letter.'

Donnell nodded. 'It was a short letter, gentlemen, but most of the details were in it. In fact, there's not much else to add.'

Shane Preston stood by the window. He'd taken the Stetson from his head, and his dark hair flopped over his high forehead.

'It's been several days now since you wrote,' said Shane. 'Any news?'

Donnell shook his head miserably. 'None.'

'So to get things straight.' Shane came right to the point. 'Your daughter left home on the westbound for Sonora, and the stage just vanished. According to your letter, the only folks who saw it were at the way-station, so something must have happened between the way-station and Sonora. When the stage didn't arrive at Sonora, your town sheriff was telegraphed and a posse went out to search. You found nothing.'

'That just about sums it up,' Ridge Donnell agreed to Shane's brief summary.

'You followed the usual stage trail?' Jonah Jones asked.

'Yes.'

'Weren't there traces of a stage leaving the trail? Wheel marks? Hoofs?'

'There was nothing.' Donnell shook his head.

32

'Absolutely nothing. All we saw were the usual rutted marks made by a hundred stagecoaches – nothing leaving the trail.'

'So there are no clues?'

Donnell stood up. He was a typical frontiersman, tall, stately, built like a buffalo around the shoulders. Yet his face was that of a man who was dying inside. Now his fists were clenched. 'You're not going to have an easy chore, Mr Preston. You'll really have to earn that thousand dollars!' Ridge Donnell's eyes leveled hard on Shane's. 'I'm presuming, of course, that you're accepting the contract?'

'Mr Donnell,' Shane Preston said wryly, 'we didn't ride all the way over here for our health.'

The door opened and Rona walked in with the tray. Shane watched as she pulled the crystal stopper from the decanter and began to pour the brandy into glasses.

'Rona, gentlemen,' Donnell said proudly, 'is my wife.' The girl smiled and old Jonah looked surprised.

'Rebecca's mother died a few years ago,' the rancher explained, 'and I remarried. Some folks said I was a fool, even called me names like 'squawman' at the time, but I never regretted marrying my Kiowa princess.'

'Thank you, Mrs. Donnell,' Shane said, accepting

his elegant glass.

The tall, rugged gunslinger felt a mite out of place sipping brandy from a balloon glass in these surroundings, but nevertheless, he sat down to enjoy his brandy. Jonah, however, was reveling in the situation and made a mock gesture of sniffing his drink before downing it in one draught in a most ungentlemanly fashion.

'More questions, Mr Preston?' the rancher asked.

'Stages can't just vanish,' Shane said. 'Didn't someone figure there could have been a hold-up?'

Donnell's fingers trembled on his brandy glass. 'There was one thing I found out after I wrote that letter,' he admitted.

'Oh?'

'There was an army payroll on that stage.'

'So if outlaws got wind of the payroll, there could have been a hold-up,' Shane mused. 'Could be the stage, and your daughter, are in outlaw hands.'

In that moment of time Shane had just voiced Donnell's unspoken fears. The rancher stood up and walked right over to Shane. 'Find her, Mr Preston!' His tortured voice was hoarse, pleading, desperate with worry. 'Bring her back to me! One thousand, two thousand, even three! Just name your price!'

'Mr Donnell,' Shane Preston said gently, 'your original fee is more than generous. But there's one thing you have to accept. Rebecca may not be still alive. We'll ride out and comb the territory for her, but you have to face that possibility.'

Donnell looked sharply away from him. Sweat was beading his brow.

'That letter you wrote to us was – well – kinda unusual,' Shane went on. 'Fact is, Mr Preston, we're not gods. Don't put all your faith in us because we managed to help your pard back in Kansas.'

'But – but you did clean up that Ringo outfit,' the rancher whispered.

Shane had been flattered by the faith Ridge Donnell had shown in his letter, but he knew it was the blind, almost unreasoning faith of a desperate man, a man grasping at straws because he loved his daughter. Now, however, was the time for cold, hard reality.

'We'll be riding out to bring back your daughter, alive if possible,' the gunfighter said slowly. 'But just remember this. Jonah and me ain't infallible, and this is one hell of a chore you've given us.'

'And,' Jonah Jones backed up his pard's summary of the situation, 'the trail's been cold some days now.'

Jonah downed his second glass of brandy and reached across for the decanter. The rancher slumped down into the soft cushions of his sofa, and Shane watched him closely. Donnell wouldn't be the first man to base his faith on the reputation which rode with the two gunslicks. Hitherto, the faith of many men had proved to be well founded, but this time things were different. Shane counted himself to be a reasonable optimist, but in this instance, he figured that the odds were indeed long.

Shane broke the silence. 'I want to move on out right away. Reckon you can arrange some chow for us to take?'

'Rona,' Donnell nodded to his Indian wife who'd been standing beside him. The woman glided from the room.

'I'll write you that check now,' Donnell said.

'No.' Shane Preston shook his head. 'If we bring your Rebecca back alive, then you can write out that check – but not before. No dice, no pay.'

Donnell stood up.

'Reckon we'll be moseying out to our horses,' Shane said. Jonah took a wistful look at the decanter but Shane grabbed the stopper and fitted it back into the lip.

'Thanks a whole lot!' Jonah said feelingly.

Shane led the way back up the hall and out into the warm sun. Leaving Jonah to bewail the brandy still untouched in the decanter, he drew the rancher aside. He lit a cigarette, listening while Donnell gave him a detailed description of his daughter's appearance.

Finally, satisfied, Shane swung into the saddle.

Rona Donnell emerged with a package of food under one arm and two canteens full of fresh water under the other. Donnell slid the food parcel into Jonah's pouch, and the two gunfighters hung the canteens over their saddlehorns.

'We hope to bring her back here, Mr Donnell,' Shane Preston said.

'I'd prefer Apache Wells,' said Donnell, unexpectedly.

'Huh?' Shane frowned.

'Where the hell's Apache Wells?' Jonah snorted.

Donnell stared up at Shane. 'It's an old mission half-way between here and Sonora, right in the middle of the desert where the trail forks to Sand Creek. I promised to meet Oliver Stobie there. He's Rebecca's intended. You see, the stage from Sonora to Sand Creek stops off at the mission to rest the horses, and it'll be dropping off Stobie to meet me there.'

'What the hell for?' Jonah asked.

Donnell flushed. 'I wrote Stobie that I was hiring you. He's the only one apart from Rona who knows you've been approached. The letter was kinda like the one I wrote to you – sorta full of faith, as you put it. By the time Stobie gets it, he'll be – well – hopeful that you two will ride into Apache Wells with his bride-to-be.'

'For cryin' out loud!' Jonah Jones exclaimed incredulously.

'So Stobie will be waiting there for her,' Shane stated. 'He'll figure he can simply collect her and ride back to Sonora for the wedding . . . just like nothing had happened? Right?'

Ridge Donnell nodded miserably.

Shane could have chided the rancher, told him he'd been a crazy fool to make near-impossible promises on behalf of two men he'd never seen before. And yet, as Shane looked into the sad eyes of the rancher, he could forgive him. Ridge Donnell was a big man in this valley, a wealthy man, a man others looked up to; maybe sometimes he was even ruthless in his business dealings. But right now Ridge Donnell was merely a scared father who'd lost his daughter, a desperate man clutching at straws. And maybe, Shane told himself, he was entitled to his blind faith.

'See you at Apache Wells,' Shane said.

The tall gunfighter wheeled Snowfire around, and followed by Jonah Jones urging his mare into a trot, Shane headed for the knife-edged pass that opened out into the wilderness.

The shadows were growing longer and the wind was sweeping over the wasteland as the gunfighters reined in on the jutting ridge of pumice overlooking the desolate red plain of shifting sand and aged, contorted rocks. Behind them, patches of purple sage dotted the wilderness, but up here the plateau was barren. Here and there desolate buttes cut the graying sky, their rounded rims tinged gold by the dying sun.

'There it is.' Shane Preston pointed out the way-station beneath them on the winding desert trail. 'The first of our two places to call on.'

Jonah grimaced and sucked in his breath. It had been a long, hard trail and the red dust plastered his hair and clung to his wrinkled skin like a blanket.

'Let's hope their liquor supply's good,' Jonah grunted, 'because we won't get over-much at the next place. Hunk ain't exactly renowned for havin' the territory's best rotgut!'

Shane jogged Snowfire down the ridge. This way-station, where the ill-fated stage had last stopped, was to be their first call. The proprietor must have been the last man to see the passengers, and Shane wanted to talk to him. Not that Shane expected to learn much, but he had to start someplace. After that, they'd set out for Hunk O'Malley's cabin on the mesa. Jonah had fought desperately against paying a social call on Hunk O'Malley, for reasons Shane understood only too well, but the tall gunhawk had over-ruled his pard's reluctance. Hunk was the only man they knew who lived in this godforsaken wilderness, and there was just a chance he might have heard something. Again, a slender possibility, but when the odds were long, a man had to investigate even the remotest trail.

At the foot of the ridge, a creek bed twisted like a dry snakeskin between marbled boulders. The riders urged their mounts over the parched bed, passing the bleached bones of a coyote. They topped the opposite bank and followed the dusty trail to the way-station looming out of the sand.

The way-station was a lonely, pine-log structure, almost a perfect square fronted by a leaning porch and two rain-barrels. Right alongside the eastern wall was a stable with twin doors banging softly in the wind.

Shane slid out of the saddle and looped his reins over the tie-rail. The older gunhawk was slower and saddle-sore, and he groaned as he levered his frame to the ground. Suddenly, the front door scraped wide.

'Howdy,' the lean streak in the doorway said cautiously. 'Seen you coming down the slope.'

Shane glanced briefly at him. The man was bald, strangely white-skinned in this country of bronzed men. His face was angular and his squinting eyes summed up the riders.

'How's your whisky, mister?' Jonah wanted to know.

This blunt question seemed to put the lean man at ease and a ghost of a smile formed over his bloodless lips.

'Good enough,' he said.

'We'll have coffee,' Shane said firmly, and Jonah screwed up his leathery face in disgust.

'Come inside.'

Shane ducked his head as he walked through the doorway and followed the thin man into the front room. The floor of the barroom was sanded, six tables lined the length of the far wall, and the shelves behind the bar counter held dusty bottles of cheap rotgut and dirty glasses. A small sign announcing ROOMS pointed towards an even lower doorway than the front one.

'Ain't much of a place,' the way-station's owner apologized. 'But we don't get enough customers to afford improvements. Just a coupla stages per week. By the way, my name's Provis.'

Shane sat down and stretched out his long legs.

'Coffee, Mr Provis,' Shane prompted him.

'Oh, sure.' Provis stalked to the low doorway. 'Elizabeth! Two cups of coffee!'

Provis took up his position behind the bar, as if half expecting them to order whisky, but Shane lit a cigarette.

41

'On the way to Sonora?' Provis asked pleasantly. He'd be in his early fifties, the tall gunslinger decided, and one of the frailest individuals Shane had come across in some time.

'Not exactly,' Shane said. 'We're looking for a stagecoach.'

Provis looked startled, then nodded his head. 'You mean, you're trying to find that vanished stage?'

'Uh huh. Heard it stopped here. You were maybe the last person to see those passengers.'

Provis ran his thumb over his Adam's apple.

'Who are you?' he demanded at last.

'A coupla riders hired by Donnell,' Jonah said.

'To find his daughter?' Provis reached for a bottle of his own rotgut. The cheap liquor gurgled into a glass. 'Hell, I wish you luck! And you'll need it, because that posse couldn't find a single trace.'

'There are two or three questions I'd like to put to you,' Shane Preston said.

'Look, gentlemen,' Provis swallowed his liquor, 'I told the possemen all I know. Sheriff Buchan, Kenning, Donnell – all of 'em. They fired a helluva lot of questions at me. I don't intend going through it all again.'

Shane drew on his cigarette. 'See anything strange happening about the time the stage was due?'

Provis hesitated. 'What do you mean?'

42

'See any riders around?'

'Riders! Hell! I hardly see a rider in weeks!' Provis downed his drink. 'This ain't Main Street, you know.'

'The stage was carrying an army payroll,' Shane pursued.

'I saw no one except the driver and the passengers,' Provis asserted. 'Definitely no riders.'

'Temptin' for outlaws, wouldn't you say?'

'Dan!' It was a woman's call from another room.

'See you in a minute,' Dan Provis said, relishing the excuse to leave them. 'Just make yourselves to home.'

The way-station man headed for the low doorway and strode down the passageway. He walked into the parlor where his wife was standing by the hot woodstove.

'Close the door!' Elizabeth Provis snapped. She was a little woman, not unlike her husband in looks, with a black birthmark on her left cheek. Thin strands of white hair betrayed her age. 'Pronto!'

Provis kicked the door shut. 'Elizabeth,' he began, 'they're – they're asking questions about the stage!'

'I heard 'em!' she whipped back at her husband. 'Sneaked a look through the door before I ran back here. Don't you know who they are?'

'Huh?' Provis scratched his bald head.

'Shane Preston and Jonah Jones!' she whispered.

Dan Provis still looked mystified.

'Don't you ever read that paper the stage drops off here once a month?' she demanded. 'The tall one had his picture in it a few months ago after they cleaned up the Jubal Clancy outfit in Laredo. I sure remember it, because there was a big story about what had happened and the kind of men hired to do the work their spooked deputies couldn't handle. Preston and Jones are hired guns, men who sell their services to the highest bidder.'

'And Donnell hired them,' Provis supplied. 'So what, Elizabeth? The posse failed, and so will these rannies.'

Elizabeth Provis lifted the kettle from the hotplate.

'From what I've read and heard about Shane Preston and Jonah Jones, they ain't put off the scent that easy.' The woman sniffed. 'I wonder if the boss knows about these riders being on the trail?'

'I reckon he'd want to know, Dan,' she continued. 'That's what he pays us for – to keep him informed!'

She spooned the crushed coffee beans into two cups.

Thick beads of sweat were standing out on her husband's brow.

'Look,' Elizabeth Provis said, 'I'll fix those two gun-hawks with their coffee. You sneak out to the stable, saddle up, and ride like hell to Boulder Bluff. Tell the

44

boss Shane Preston and Jonah Jones are here asking questions and we told them nothing. Reckon the boss will take things from there. He mightn't do anything, but I reckon he oughta know two of the territory's toughest gunslingers have been hired by Donnell and they're snooping around.'

'Yeah,' Provis said miserably.

'Saddle up,' Elizabeth directed him coldly. 'And don't let them hear you ride off. Meantime, I'll tell them you had to check your traps and I'll be serving them.'

Provis grabbed his Stetson and jammed it on his head. He plunged out of the back doorway, moving swiftly through the soft sand to the stable doors. They whined as he shoved them open. His bay gelding was in its stall, white-eyed in the gloom. Provis was breathing heavily as he hauled the saddle from its wall-hook. It was a long ride to Boulder Bluff, but he knew the journey was essential. The man who secretly led the Long Knife outfit paid well for information on the freight the stages carried, and it was easy money for Elizabeth and himself. He didn't want to jeopardize the arrangement by neglecting to pass on the news, bad as it was. He tightened the cinch and led the gelding out into the stillness of late afternoon. He walked the horse down-trail, making sure that the sound of hoofs was muffled by the soft sand. At length, where the trail dipped out of sight of the way-station, he mounted up. Provis raked his spurs across the gelding's sides and it stretched into a lope. It would be the middle of the night before he saw the lights of Boulder Bluff.

THREE

SHADOWS IN THE DESERT

'Hunk O'Malley!' Jonah gulped out the name for about the tenth time. 'Hell, Shane! That's one *hombre* I just don't want to ride over to see!'

Shane lit his cigarette and the flare illuminated his head and shoulders against the canvas of gathering dusk. There was a wide grin on his face.

'Heck!' Jonah spelled out his objection to the visit. 'That dang blasted sister he lives with – she spooks me!'

'We ain't riding over to see Ada,' Shane told him, blowing out the match. 'I want to talk to Hunk.'

'But that fat barrel of a female will be there,' Jonah Jones complained. 'And you remember what happened last time we called over there. Doggone it, Shane! She actually wanted me to . . . hell! Kiss her!'

'But you managed to resist the temptation,' Shane Preston reminded him wryly.

'I happened to run fast enough,' Jonah corrected him.

Shane drew on his cigarette.

'Jonah,' he said seriously. 'Hunk's our only chance. We drew a blank at the way-station, and it seems like there's just one place left to ride over and ask questions. Hunk O'Malley's cabin. An old desert rat like him knows most things that go on in the wilderness, and he might just have heard about the stage.'

Jonah snorted, unconvinced.

'Anyway,' Shane went on, 'we haven't called on Hunk and Ada for over a year, and they are your friends.'

'Hunk is,' Jonah grunted his amendment.

Shane smiled as he contemplated the old desert prospector he planned on visiting. Fat, pot-bellied, Hunk wasn't exactly a striking figure of a man. In fact, some described him as plain ugly, and Ada was in the same category. The incredible fact was that once O'Malley had been a banker, but he'd forsaken the life of hustle and responsibility for the uncertain existence of a prospector. It was while panning for gold that O'Malley and his sister had met up with Jonah. Three years ago Hunk and Ada had left their diggings to live in this wilderness, and since then the two gunslingers had visited them but twice. Now was as good a time as any to make a third social call. Last time Hunk had dominated the conversation with tales and legends of the desert, and Shane only hoped that he'd heard something of the lost stage.

Jonah was still mumbling his objections into his shaggy white beard.

'It's a long ride to the mesa,' Shane said. 'Reckon we'll waste no more time.'

He spoke softly to Snowfire and the stallion responded instantly, surging forward for the dim outline of the mesa slopes. Jonah muttered a last curse and joined him. Together they rode in the cool-ness. Soon the grayness of dusk surrendered to the blanket of darkness that covered the silent desert. A vague moon rose as the last crimson streak faded in the western sky, and as the riders approached the mesa slopes, the eerie moonlight bathed the cold sands. They reined in beneath the towering mesa, looking up at the stark black walls of pumice steeping upwards into the void. After resting their horses for awhile, the gunfighters headed up through a twisting, narrow pass.

The mesa was a vast elevated table of flat rock, a huge expanse of sage and mesquite. Reining in, the riders let their eyes rove to the northern limits. Drenched in moonlight, this tableland of rock and sand was broken only by strange, stunted rocks that stood up like blackened teeth. An awesome silence gripped the mesa, and Jonah suppressed a shiver.

'This is one helluva place to live, Shane,' the older gunhawk complained.

They pushed further, on.

Suddenly Shane halted Snowfire and at once Jonah reined in, too. The tall gunslinger's hand dropped to his six-gun, and moments later the shadows ahead on the trail moved.

There were three of them: vague spectral figures, riders blending into horses. One of them rode out from beneath the dead branches of a skeleton cottonwood, and Shane thumbed back the hammer of his gun.

'Damn 'breeds!' Jonah spat in disgust. 'Worse than coyotes!'

They were silhouetted against the moonlight, ragged, unkempt and dark. One of them wore a cavalry uniform. The tallest 'breed, his hair flowing black and free over his shoulders, prodded his pony a little closer.

'For Pete's sake!' Jonah's brow was beaded with

perspiration. 'Why the hell don't they come at us?'

'Right now we're being sized up,' Shane Preston said softly. 'Keep your hand on your gun.'

The tall 'breed broke away from the others, leaving them beside the dead cottonwood. Slowly, deliberately, he rode his pinto pony towards the stunted rock that protruded to the right of the two gunfighters. Shane's gaze followed him warily, and finally the man reined in and surveyed the desert travelers with hawk-like eyes.

The half-breed wearing the oversize bluecoat uniform started to head around to Shane's left.

'So that's their game,' Shane murmured. 'They figure on circling us and trapping us in a crossfire.'

Jonah's hand gripped his gun.

'Hell, Shane!' he croaked. 'Are we just gonna sit here like rats in a trap?'

'We ride,' Shane said under his breath. 'Straight for the one by the cottonwood – nice and slow.'

'OK.' Jonah kicked Tessie into a walk and the half-breed hovering close to the old tree began to waver. The renegade jabbered something to his companions and the tall 'breed beside the stunted rock let out a yell. With a harsh cry, the rangy half-breed whipped his rifle into play, aiming it at Shane.

The silence of the mesa was shattered by the roar of Shane's black six-gun booming a split second before the lean 'breed's long finger found the trigger. The renegade lurched forward, screaming with rage and pain. His rifle slithered down over his pony's back, and there was a dull thud as the 'breed followed his gun into the mesa's dust.

Momentarily the other ragged riders stared at their fallen companion, and then the breed in the cavalry shirt wheeled his pony around.

Relentlessly, the two gunfighters bore down towards the cottonwood. The 'breed rider there gesticulated wildly, screeching at the man who was heading away into the safety of the night. Jonah's gun thundered and the lead smashed the man's shoulder. The hapless 'breed fell forward, clutching frantically at his pony's mane. He kicked his mount around the cottonwood and rode hard into the desert with Jonah pumping bullets in his wake. Shane restrained the older gunslinger with a word, and mumbling, Jonah holstered his six-gun.

Shane headed over to the fallen half-breed, and as he approached the shadow of the rock, the thin bony pony edged fearfully away. He slid from his saddle and turned the man face up.

There was a dark smudge in the center of the 'breed's shirt, a sharp tear in the fabric where Shane's bullet had ripped its way through. Shane bent down beside him. The half-breed's eyes were open and glassy in the peaceful stillness of death. Jonah's shadow fell over him.

'A half-breed sure enough,' Shane said. 'And by the looks of him, part-Kiowa.'

'What the hell's that around his neck?' Jonah growled.

Shane stood up. 'Looks like a necklace of bones.'

Jonah Jones shivered and looked around anxiously at the circle of darkness. Somewhere out there, a coyote was baying a mournful dirge.

'I don't like it, Shane,' Jonah sniffed uneasily. 'Two of those devils got away, and that means they might come back and bring others with them.'

Shane walked to Snowfire and mounted up.

'Let's get to Hunk's,' he said.

They headed away from the stunted rock, leaving the body for the 'breeds who would return for it. Rounding the cottonwood, they urged their horses into a gallop and the mesa swallowed them up.

An hour passed as the riders crossed the vast, lonesome tableland. The wind began to lash their faces and stir up tall spirals of dust that groped for the moon. For awhile, the mesa seemed to slope gradually downwards, but then, quite suddenly, the surface broke up into a hundred small, crooked ridges. Here the rocks were loose and the horses' hoofs slipped between layers of treacherous pumice. Once the gunfighters were forced to dismount and walk their horses, but soon they were in the saddle again, heading swiftly for the lone light that burned like a beacon beyond the crest of the next gentle rise.

Hunk O'Malley's cabin.

Shane and Jonah topped the rise, slowing their horses as the flickering light loomed closer and its glow framed a crude structure of baked mud and wooden window frames. There was a cock-eyed chimney protruding from the tin roof and blue-gray smoke was curling languidly into the void until the wind caught the column and whisked it away. A dog barked. The curtains moved almost imperceptibly at the front window and the two gunfighters reined in just beyond the lop-sided wooden porch.

'Howdy, howdy!' Hunk O'Malley's booming voice rang out like thunder as he shoved open the creaking door. 'Hey, Ada! Come on out here! It's Shane and Jonah!'

The two big barrel-shaped figures of brother and sister fairly leaped at their visitors. Hands were shaken, backs slapped in a hearty frontier welcome. Ada even threw her fat arms around the spluttering, protesting Jonah and gave him a wet mouthed kiss which he promptly wiped from his bruised lips with the back of his hand. For fully five minutes, the O'Malleys exchanged greetings with the riders while horses were unsaddled and stabled. Then the gun-fighters were ushered inside, and recalling last time when he'd suffered a clout to his forehead, Shane ducked very low when he entered the low doorway. Even inside, the roof was so low it was far more comfortable for Shane Preston to sit down.

'Ada,' Hunk O'Malley grinned through his bushy whiskers. 'Fetch our guests some chow.'

Ada smiled at Jonah and the white-bearded gunhawk averted his gaze.

'Well, now,' Hunk said. 'What are you two galoots doing in this corner of the desert?'

Shane rolled a fresh cigarette. 'This ain't just a social call, Hunk,' he said seriously.

'Figured it wasn't,' O'Malley shrugged.

'In fact, Hunk,' Shane said bluntly, 'we're here for some information.'

O'Malley frowned. 'What sort of information, Shane?'

'Hunk,' the tall gunfighter said, 'you once told us that nothing much happens in this desert that you don't hear about.'

'I keep my big ears to the ground,' O'Malley agreed.

'Outsiders like Jonah and me just see sand when we ride this wilderness,' Shane continued. 'But you see more. You hear more. Desert folks call on you and pass the time of day.'

'What sort of information?' Hunk repeated.

'Hunk,' Shane said earnestly, lighting his cigarette, 'we're looking for a lost stage.'

There was a long silence. Ada looked around sharply from the food closet and Hunk O'Malley's fingers beat out a steady tattoo on the table-top.

'I'll fix some coffee as well as chow,' Ada O'Malley said.

Shane drew on his cigarette. 'What have you heard, Hunk?'

O'Malley stood up and adjusted the wick of the flickering oil lamp.

'I don't hear everything that goes on,' the desert rat said. 'Tell me more.'

'It was the westbound from Boulder Bluff,' Shane said. 'Called in at the way-station, then vanished without a trace. What's the desert rumor, Hunk? There must be talk.'

Ada placed a plate of hot biscuits on the table. Jonah sniffed them and when he looked up, he saw the buxom woman's big saucer eyes staring brightly at him.

'Been a long time, Jonah,' Ada said. 'Always talking about you, I am. Ask Hunk – he'll tell you.'

'Yeah, that's right!' Hunk seemed pleased to grasp this opportunity to change the subject. 'There's no doubt about it, Jonah. Ada mentions you just about every day.'

Jonah gulped.

Ada turned to the mirror and smoothed down the black strands of her hair. Built like a buffalo, she had a rotund face with fat lips and a beaked nose. Her big bosom pushed against her gingham dress and her arms were like two octopus tentacles.

'We were talking about the stage, Hunk,' Shane Preston prompted him.

'Knowing you two galoots, Shane,' Hunk O'Malley murmured, 'you ain't riding on this job for your health. Someone's paying you.'

'Ridge Donnell.'

Hunk O'Malley whistled.

'It's his daughter who's missing on that stage.'

'If Donnell's paying you, then you're working for real paydirt!' O'Malley grunted.

Shane could read the wizened recluse like a book. He extracted a leather wallet from his hip-pocket, and while Hunk and Ada watched wide-eyed, he drew out more money than they'd seen for many a long day.

'Fifty bucks,' Shane said. 'It's yours if you start remembering some of those desert rumors you must have heard.'

'I never said I'd heard anything!' protested O'Malley.

'Fifty bucks,' Shane said.

O'Malley leaned forward. 'Old Jacob Magg called in just yesterday. Magg's a prospector, you know. Real old-timer, but he keeps his eyes and ears open. We swapped yarns over coffee and he told me about this wrecked stage in Black Goose Canyon.'

'Where's that?'

'West of the mesa. Hardly anyone ever goes, there – just a few prospectors like Magg who still figure there's gold in that dry creek bed.'

'What else did he say?'

'Nothing much. He only saw it from a distance. Didn't bother to ride close up.'

'Black Goose Canyon, huh,' mused Shane.

'Shane!' Hunk raised a warning finger. 'Now I know you two boys ain't greenhorns with guns, but you'd be dang fools to ride over to that canyon.'

'Oh?'

'It's one of Trauba's haunts,' O'Malley explained. 'Trauba leads a bunch of renegade 'breeds. Now, they leave me alone, just like they leave most folks alone who actually live in this wilderness, but they'd attack outsiders like yourselves.'

'We've already had a taste of their hospitality,' Shane said wryly. 'Three 'breeds tried to kill us a short while back. We managed to get one of them and the others quit.'

'Helluva 'breed, the one Shane killed,' Jonah contributed. 'Wore a necklace of bones.'

'A necklace of bones!' Hunk exclaimed. 'That can only be one man.'

'They all look the same to me,' Shane shrugged.

'Must have been Antonio – Trauba's son,' Hunk O'Malley said slowly. 'By hell, you got Trauba's boy!'

'And two of the buzzards got away,' Jonah grimaced.

'They'll be back with the whole outfit,' Hunk warned. 'You'd be crazy to go on!'

Shane shook his head. 'We came here to do a job, Hunk. Could this Trauba have held up the stage?'

'Shouldn't think so. Trauba's 'breeds are like buzzards with lonely travelers, but as far as I've heard, they've never taken a stage. But one outfit might.'

'What's the outfit?' Shane demanded.

'The Long Knife bunch,' Hunk said without hesitation. 'Big bunch of killers. Not 'breeds, not Indians, but white renegades. Mightn't be them, of course, but they'd be my pick.'

'And where does this Long Knife outfit hole up?'

O'Malley spread his hands. 'That's one question I don't know the answer to.'

Coffee was brought to them. Outside the rising wind lashed sand and dust against the primitive cabin like hail. Despite Hunk's continual adjustments, the lamp flickered wildly in the draughts which came through the cracks in the walls.

Cards were brought out after supper. Hunk gambled and lost ten of his fifty dollars, then decided to call it a night. Shane unrolled his blanket and prepared to bed down on the floor. Tomorrow, at sunup, they'd be on the trail to Black Goose Canyon. Jonah started to try and talk his partner into sleeping out.

Ada giggled from her room. Jonah headed for the door.

Shane said with mock sternness, 'Where's your manhood, Jones?'

Almost immediately, Ada emerged from her room clad in an enormous nightgown fringed with lace. It was so dusty that this must have been the first time she'd worn it in years. Ada's heavy hand clamped down on Jonah's shoulder.

'Been waiting a long time for you to stay the night, Jonah!' she chuckled.

Like a lamb being led to the slaughter, Jonah was propelled, into the darkness of her bedroom. Ada kicked the door shut. Shane heard his pard utter a few words of protest, and then there was a long ominous silence.

Hunk had gone off to his room. Shane lay down and rolled himself in his blanket. Outside, the stable door was banging in the wind, and somehow it

60

reminded him of another door banging, long ago. Shane fumbled for his tobacco sack in the dark and built a cigarette, remembering the reason why he'd become a gunslinger, a wandering rider who hired out his gun to the highest bidder. Once, he'd been a rancher with a small spread. He'd had a wife, a future, a home. But one day he'd ridden back to a banging door, his front door swinging in the wind, the house wide-open just as the outlaws had left it. He'd crashed inside, waded through the furniture wreckage to find the bloodied body of his young wife. While he'd been in town, outlaws had raided his spread, stolen money and property and killed the woman he loved. Overcome with grief and fury, he'd trailed them, finally to find them in a remote border saloon. He'd blasted a fat outlaw to death while the man stood guffawing at the bar counter, but even as he turned towards the second killer, the hot knife of a slug ripped open his belly. He'd folded, but before he blacked out, he caught a glimpse of the man's face, his strange insane eyes, the ugly scar down his left cheek. It was a face he'd never forget, a face that haunted him, goaded him on the lonely trails. Later, when he'd come to, he found himself bandaged and lying by a campfire with old Jonah Jones fussing over him. The oldster had taken him from the saloon, tended him, and from then onwards, the two became saddlepards.

Shane stubbed his cigarette in the sand of the floor and listened to the wild music of the rising wind.

Now he rode as a gunfighter, a man who hired out his gun for cash. He was a man who lived for one moment – the day he would meet Scarface and kill him!

Until then, the money he earned enabled him to keep himself, and the trails he rode led him into the kind of circles Scarface would be travelling. Someday, somewhere, their trails would cross. And then Shane Preston would kill for the last time.

They headed away from Hunk O'Malley's cabin as the first gray light of day fingered the eastern rims of the mesa. The night wind had dropped, and now all was stillness.

Shane and Jonah rode westward in the silence of sunup.

Right here, the terrain was almost completely flat. Only the stunted rocks broke the horizon, and here and there, beds of scented sage matted the sand.

Soon, however, the surface of the mesa began to break up. Thin ridges protruded. Hollows were scooped out of the tableland like a hundred saucers, and to the west, deep clefts showed the presence of twisting ravines.

Shane reined in Snowfire and Jonah drew alongside.

'Which one's Black Goose Canyon?' the oldster demanded.

Shane grinned. 'Early this morning, while you were still cavorting with his sister, Hunk drew me a rough map. Black Goose is right below the mesa, and we ride down to it through the gulch that's just beyond Angel's Butte.'

'Cavorting!' Jonah's face was a vivid, indignant red. 'Heck, Shane! I only slept with that dragon to keep her brother on our side!'

'Of course,' Shane Preston complimented him. 'And it was a right noble act, Jonah.'

The oldster snorted.

'By the way . . .' Shane's voice changed. 'Don't look back now, but we've got company.'

Jonah became grim. 'How many?'

'Just one. Been following us for some time now,' Shane murmured. 'One of our 'breed friends from last night, maybe.'

Jonah let out a muffled curse.

'Keep looking straight ahead,' Shane warned him sharply. 'I don't want that 'breed to know we're alerted. Two of those devils got away from us last night, and I reckon the wounded one's headed out to find Trauba.'

'And this galoot's trailing us to make sure we don't slip away,' Jonah guessed. 'He's probably leaving a damn easy trail for the rest of them to follow.'

The gunfighters headed towards the towering pumice butte. Shane didn't need to look back to know that the shadow was following. The half-breed in the army shirt had been trailing them since they left the cabin.

FOUR

THE CANYON OF DEAD MEN

The gulch was a thin slit in the mesa, a deep gorge sliced out of the pumice that dropped even lower to a valley of red sand. An ancient Indian trail steeped down into the ravine, and the two gunfighters headed slowly and tortuously along this crumbling trail that clung to the gorge's wall like an eyebrow. Shane led the way, with Jonah walking Tessie at his heels. Shane looked back just once, casually. Sure enough, their shadow was right behind them.

They reached the floor of the gorge. Sheer, contorted walls rose on both sides and the towering peaks cut out the warmth of early morning. Down here, the shadows were dark and a dampness pervaded the air. The gorge dropped in a dozen stairs of slippery rock. Now even Shane had to dismount to walk his horse.

The gunfighters pushed further into the bowels of the gorge. The two walls almost joined but suddenly opened out onto a high, tree-lined rim that overlooked a vast canyon stretching as far as the eye could see.

Black Goose Canyon was an awesome valley carved out of strange black rocks that rose to the pale sky like the fingers of veined hands. The floor of the valley was all sand broken only by a patch of flowering sagebrush and three dead trees that stood alone just below the rim. The gunslingers reined in and buzzards floated from one of the peaks to perch on the ridge that presided over the pass. Jonah suppressed an involuntary shiver as one of the scavenger birds let out a raucous croak, and he dropped his hand to his six-shooter. Shane restrained him, riding forward to the very edge of the rim. A heavy silence pervaded the canyon. Nothing moved. No breath of wind stirred the sand.

Shane's eyes roved over the basin. At first all they saw was the red sand and the black pinnacles. Then the gunhawk spotted a distant object which might have been the wreck.

'Under the tall ridge,' Shane pointed out the black slab wedged between two needles of pumice.

'Hell!' Jonah exclaimed. 'They must have rolled the stage over the edge!'

'So we ride down and take a look-see.'

'Shane,' the older rider said softly. 'How about our 'breed friend?'

'We'll take a closer look at the stage and then deal with him,' Shane Preston said. 'Fact is, I'm kinda glad he's behind us because I've a feeling he's gonna come in useful.'

'Huh?' Jonah gaped.

But Shane was already prodding his white palomino down from the rim. Soon Snowfire's hoofs were making a trail in the soft sand, and as he rode across the open space, a feeling of desolation gripped him. Out here, in the center of Black Goose Canyon, a man felt insignificant, vulnerable, with the dark, forbidding walls staring down. Slowly, the wrecked stagecoach rose out of the sand like the ghostly wreck of an old galleon in a rolling sea. The gunfighters rode closer. Smashed wood panels protruded from the sand where they'd been thrown after the impact of the fall. A broken wheel was silted over with fine sand and splinters of wood littered the canyon floor. The stage itself was merely a skeleton sticking out of the redness, shreds of ruptured wood clinging to a twisted frame. Only two wheels remained on a broken axle and the coach's seat had been tossed clear. Shane glanced up at the ridge. It was directly overhead, its knife-edge scarred by the spinning wheels of the stage just before it made its final plunge into the canyon.

'Shane!' Jonah had dismounted on the other side of the wreck.

Shane slipped out of his saddle.

'Reckon this is where they buried the passengers,' Jonah said soberly, pointing to three low mounds of sand.

Shane looked quickly over his shoulder at the pass. A speck was riding onto the big rim.

'Let's find out who they are, Jonah,' Shane Preston said.

'How come?' Alarm registered on Jonah's wizened face.

'We dig open these graves. Reckon they'll be real shallow, so we won't have far to go. Probably we can do it with our hands.'

Jonah Jones gulped. 'Open graves?'

'How the hell else are we gonna find out whether Rebecca is here or not?'

'Ain't that obvious?' Jonah sniffed.

'There were four folks on the westbound,' Shane

said, bending down to scoop away the sand from the first mound. 'A driver, two soldiers and Rebecca. There seems to be only three graves.'

The gunfighters scooped and shoveled away the sand from two of the mounds. A lone buzzard wheeled overhead as if in anticipation of a feast. Shane's hand delved deeper into the sand, and suddenly his fingers felt hardness. He dug away more sand and then a faded piece of blue fabric showed, and he could smell the strong, stinking odor of decomposed flesh.

'This one's a soldier,' Shane said.

'So's mine,' Jonah turned his face away from the hole he'd scooped out.

'We'll check out the last one.'

'How about that 'breed-boy?'

'He's watching from the rim.'

Kneeling by the last mound, the two gunhawks opened up the grave. This one was a little deeper than the others, but finally Shane's long fingers found an arm. They shoveled away more sand.

'Reckon this one's the stage driver, Jonah,' Shane observed. 'Leastways, he's a man.'

'And Rebecca?'

'Like I warned Donnell,' Shane said bluntly. 'I reckon the outlaws have her.'

'Then she's still alive.'

'Maybe it'd be better if she weren't. Figured from the start this could have happened. She's young, and from all accounts, pretty. Outlaws living so far from women and home comforts wouldn't kill a prize like Rebecca Donnell.'

'Then she's maybe in some outlaw's camp? Long Knife's, huh?'

'We don't know for sure the Long Knife outfit was responsible,' the tall gunfighter shrugged. 'But Hunk seemed to figure it could only have been them. Mind you, there's only one way to find out. Take a ride to Long Knife's camp.'

Jonah stared at him. 'You loco?'

'Hunk didn't know where the Long Knife outfit holed up,' Shane mused. 'But I figure there's someone around who might.'

Shane's eyes were on a narrow opening between two black pinnacles, a thin, steep pass that led out of Black Goose Canyon and back to the mesa.

'Cover up these bodies again,' Shane said. 'We've some riding to do.'

They began to push the sand back over the rotting flesh and, cheated, the wheeling buzzard fluttered back to a peak. The sun was mounting the azure sky and myriads of flies buzzed around as the gunslingers completed their grisly chore.

'That someone who might help us find the camp,'

Jonah ventured. 'You mean the 'breed?'

'We might as well make use of him,' Shane said. 'I reckon one of Trauba's renegades will know where another outlaw band holes up.'

They strode to their horses.

Heading away from the remains of the stagecoach, the gunslingers set their faces at the small mouth of the pass beneath the twin needles of rock.

They rode into the shadows of the spiraling pumice monuments. A hot breeze met them at the entrance to the passage, and urging their horses, the gunslingers moved swiftly upwards into the pass. Here, jumbled rocks and cave-lined ridges stared down at the riders as they mounted the steep slope to the mesa's crest. Shane led the way, suddenly reining in Snowfire when a thin ledge rose from the rock floor and groped upwards to the dark, gaping jaws of a cave.

'Hide the horses, Jonah,' Shane said as he eased himself out of the saddle. 'Then stake out on the other side. I'll be in the cave. When our 'breed friend shows, remember one thing. I want him alive.'

Jonah Jones nodded, leaning over to take the palomino's reins.

Shane stalked to the foot of the ledge. He levered his lean frame up onto the eyebrow trail, his boots treading the broken rock. Standing up, he flattened his back to the sheer rock face and edged himself along the jutting rim. Finally he ducked into the darkness of the musty cave. Just below him was the floor of the pass, a twisting snake of pumice that spilled out onto the flat mesa. He glanced over at the opposite wall of the pass. Jonah had led the horses behind a huge, bald boulder, and now his heavy figure was trying to squeeze into a crevice.

A deep hush gripped the passage.

Shane crouched low and slipped the six-shooter from his holster.

By now, Jonah had managed to back right into the crevice, and from his elevation, all Shane could see was the battered rim of the oldster's Stetson.

Presently he heard the muffled sound of unshod hoofs on hard pumice. Shane edged to the mouth of the cave, his six-shooter poised. Moments later the 'breed rounded the bend in the pass. His wiry pony came closer. Just below the cave, the trail dipped, and the 'breed slowed his mount to a walk. Shane crawled onto the ledge, his chest flat to the rock.

'Hold it!' Shane's harsh command echoed out over the pass. 'Hold it or you die!'

The half-breed froze, halting his pony in its tracks. Scared, pale eyes were lifted slowly to the ledge, meeting the cold gray eyes of the man who held the six-shooter.

'Now do like I say, 'breed-boy,' Shane drawled. 'Climb down from that pony and stand with your hands high.'

'Please – please – what is this?' the half-breed bleated.

'You know damn well what this is,' Shane said. 'You were one of those bastards who tried to kill us last night. It so happened we got Trauba's son, so while your pard's gone to fetch the whole bunch, you've been trailing us. Well, maybe it's a good thing you came along. Get down!'

The half-breed let his eyes drop to the gun stuck in his belt, but glancing up at the gaping muzzle of Shane's six-gun, he decided against any tricks. He slid from the pony's back, raising his hands as Jonah forced his way out of the crevice and jabbed a rifle into his ribs. Jonah relieved him of his gun, whipping it out of his belt and stuffing it into his own. Shane climbed down and paced over to the 'breed.

'What's your name?' he demanded.

Momentarily the fear left the captive's eyes and he surveyed Shane with an insolent stare.

'My name is Femo – and you are both fools!' he snarled. He was a lithe, olive-skinned individual, and Shane judged him to be part-Mexican, part-Indian. Flashing eyes lit up as the 'breed smiled. 'Soon Trauba will kill you both! *Sí*, soon you both get staked out over ant-hills – that is the way Trauba deals with your kind!'

'Sounds a right pleasant character,' Jonah quipped.

'Maybe Trauba uses ant-hills,' Shane said wryly. 'But we use different methods. Jonah, take him to the mesa. Reckon we'll find a nice tall tree there.'

A flicker of fear passed through Femo as he stared at the hard, unrelenting face of Shane Preston.

'You heard him!' Jonah Jones cracked, grinding the gun muzzle into the half-breed's back. 'Walk!'

Shane collected the horses while his pard prodded the protesting Femo through the pass. The half-breed was jabbering away in Spanish but the gunslingers paid no heed to him. He was marched out of the pass, and once on the mesa, was shoved towards a towering old cedar.

'Reckon this'll do us,' Shane said as they halted in the shadow of the tree. He uncoiled the rope which hung from his saddlehorn, tied a noose and tossed the rope over a low branch. 'Now, Femo, this is what you call white man's justice. You're an outlaw, one of Trauba's murdering outfit, and this is an execution. Savvy?'

'No!' pleaded the half-breed miserably. 'Please – no!'

'Sit him on his pony, Jonah.'

74

Grabbing Femo by the collar of his tattered shirt, Jonah half-lifted, half-shoved him onto the pony's back. Femo's eyes dilated as Shane dropped the noose over his head and began to tighten it around his neck. He started to blubber away in Spanish, but apparently, Shane paid no heed.

'Just to let you in on what's gonna happen in a few moments, Femo,' Shane said casually. 'We slap your pony on the rump and it gallops forward, leaving you dancing on air. Not such a slow death as staked out over an ant-hill, mind, but I reckon it'll do for you.'

'Señor! Please! Femo will do anything! Femo does not want to die! Please!'

'Mind, Femo,' Shane said with a shrug as he reached for his tobacco sack, 'there is just something you could do which'd make me cut you down.'

'Señor, name it, name it!'

'You could take me someplace,' Shane said, rolling his cigarette.

'*Sí, sí, señor*! Anyplace!'

'My pard and me are headed for Long Knife's camp,' Shane said deliberately.

There was a long silence.

'You see, Femo, we figure an outlaw like you is sure to know where a bunch of fellow-owlhoots hole up, especially a bunch as tough as Long Knife's!'

'I have not even heard of this – this Long Knife,'

Femo stammered.

'Bad luck,' Shane said, striking a match. 'Jonah, get ready to slap his pony.'

'No! No!' Femo's voice was high-pitched, hysterical.

'Fact is, Femo,' Shane said, 'if you ain't gonna be of any use to us, we might as well get the hangin' over with right here and now. OK, Jonah?'

Jonah nodded soberly and advanced towards the pony's rump. The pony shifted slightly and the rope bit into Femo's oily-skinned neck.

'I know of Long Knife!' Femo screamed frantically.

Shane lit his cigarette. 'Then you'll take us to his camp.'

Femo hesitated, and Shane could see the cold fear mount once again in the 'breed's eyes.

'Seems to me you got a choice, Femo,' Shane said dryly. 'Either hang now or get killed by Long Knife later. If I was in your boots, I'd choose to keep on breathing a little while longer.'

Femo swallowed.

'I take you there, *señors*,' he said.

FIVE

OUTLAW'S WOMAN

The room stank.

It was dark and dreary, with sacking nailed across the windows where once panes of glass had sat. In the center of the room was a dirty table upon which were stacked the soiled dishes left over from the noon meal.

Rebecca let her eyes move over the far wall. The hooks hammered into the timber held up Jeb Ryan's clothes – Levis, shirts, underwear, socks – the clothes she was expected to wash for him. And that wasn't to be her only chore. She had to cook for Ryan and the others, taking turns with Honey Anne, the strange woman she'd found in this outlaw camp.

And that wasn't all. Tonight she had to sleep with Ryan, just as she had done ever since they'd arrived at this wilderness camp. The very memory of his hot, sweaty flesh and his alcohol-laden breath made her sick in the stomach, but she knew that she had no choice. She was Jeb Ryan's woman.

Rebecca stood up and walked slowly over to the broken mirror that hung on the wall. She looked at herself and drew in her breath. The once silky-black hair was dirty and unkempt; her soft skin had been hardened and lined by the ordeal she'd suffered; and now, suddenly, she looked ten years older than her twenty-two years. Her fingers strayed to the neck of her dress. It was torn, violated by greedy hands, and some of the buttons were missing. Those buttons still lay buried in the sand where her innocence had been brutally assailed by four coarse men who'd later taken her back to their camp. Now, however, she was safe from the attentions of three of them. Jeb Ryan had claimed her as his own.

'Nearly chow-time, Rebecca.'

She hadn't noticed the door opening, but now she turned as Honey Anne walked inside.

'Is it?' Rebecca's tone was disinterested.

'Hell, Rebecca!' Honey Anne's language was as coarse as the outlaws'. 'You damn well got to eat, or we'll be burying you.'

'Maybe that'd be better than this,' she said.

Honey Anne came over and placed her right hand

on Rebecca's shoulder. Looking at her in the mirror, Rebecca saw a face which once must have been beautiful. Long, blonde hair straggled down past an oval face highlighted by deep blue eyes that somehow seemed to hold an eternal, melancholy expression. Once, Honey Anne had been a saloon queen, and once, Rebecca surmised, she would have turned a hundred heads on any street.

'Been meaning to have a talk with you, Rebecca,' Honey Anne said softly.

'What's there to talk about?' Rebecca shrugged.

'You.'

Rebecca glanced out the door. The camp was an abandoned outpost once staffed by a platoon of soldiers, a crumbling adobe-lined fort erected in the desert by an army long-gone. From this room, she could see the remains of the western wall which was now stained crimson by the setting sun. Right in the middle of the old parade-ground was a fire, and she could make out the four figures which stood around its warmth, awaiting supper.

'You see, Rebecca,' the ex-saloon queen said. 'I kinda know how you feel.'

'Oh?'

'I was once in your position,' Honey Anne recounted. 'In fact, it was five years ago yesterday that I was taken from a stage, just like you were. Did the

79

boys tell you about it?'

Rebecca shook her head.

'They held up the stage going to Sand Creek,' Honey Anne said. 'I was the only passenger and they took me. At the time I was on my way to work in the Lucky Deuce in Sand Creek. They brought me here, made me wash and cook for them, only I'm not so lucky as you.'

'What do you mean'

'Jeb's claimed you,' Honey Anne said. 'I've always belonged to them all. I don't have to spell out what that means, Rebecca.'

Rebecca swallowed. 'Have you ever tried to escape?'

'Escape! Where to? Out there is the desert, and death. It's safer here.'

'You said it was supper-time.'

They walked outside into the gathering dusk. The ancient outpost was set on a hill of rock, a square-walled fort that overlooked the desert sands. Once, the military had maintained a post here to keep the ravaging Kiowas under control. Twice, the Indians had massacred the soldiers and their wives, and twenty years ago strategy demanded that the fort be abandoned. The desert almost claimed the walls and buildings, and when the outlaws took over, they had to shovel away the sand to use the buildings.

'Well, well!' Jeb Ryan grinned. 'She's decided to have chow with us. Looks like she's coming around, boys!'

'About time,' Brett Dayman growled. He was a thin-faced outlaw with a glass eye. Once a lawman, he'd turned killer when he discovered that an outlaw's paydirt was more than treble the paltry wages they gave him for wearing a badge. 'Here – serve me some soup.'

They watched as Rebecca stooped down to ladle out the beef-soup Honey Anne had brewed for them. She was conscious of their stares, and she pulled her dress together where the buttons had been torn off.

'What do we do with her next week?' Wes Morrender demanded.

Ryan shrugged. 'She'll stay here.'

Wes Morrender frowned. He had a bushy red beard and a head that was completely bald. Rebecca had learned that Morrender had once been a bounty hunter.

'We'll be away a coupla days,' Morrender reminded Ryan. 'Taking the Sand Creek bank won't be no five minute job.'

'Don't worry,' Jeb assured him. 'Rebecca knows damn well that outside this fort she'd die. Starvation, snakes, half-breeds like Trauba's bunch. She'll be staying. Right, Rebecca?'

Ryan's cruel fingers held her arm in a vice-like grip. The girl nodded.

Rodd Lewis, the other member of the outfit, stirred the fire and passed his plate over to Rebecca. She met his eyes, noted the same fire in them that she'd seen ever since coming here. Lewis was one member of the gang who resented Jeb's claim to her.

Rebecca ladled out soup for herself. At first she'd refused to eat, but sheer hunger had forced her to change her mind two days ago. She sat down, listening in silence as the outlaws exchanged small talk. Darkness was enclosing the outpost like a giant black hand. Soon the wilderness beyond was merely a dark mysterious void and the world narrowed to this glowing campfire.

Supper over, Rebecca walked back to the room she shared with Jeb Ryan. She lit the oil lamp and stood there looking at the crude wooden bed. At this moment she was thinking of the man she loved, Oliver Stobie. Before the intended wedding, she'd kept herself for him. Oliver was to have been her first and only man. Now she was a misused outlaw's woman. No tears came to her eyes. The time for tears had passed, and like Honey Anne, she was becoming resigned to her fate.

Two hours passed. Outside, the men were drinking and playing cards. Honey Anne came in to talk to her before retiring to the adjacent room.

'Rebecca,' she said softly as they both watched the

card-players gulping their stolen rotgut. 'Don't get the wrong idea about me.'

'What do you mean?'

'I told you how it's been with me since coming here,' Honey Anne said. 'I didn't say I liked it. In fact, I hate their guts!'

With that, the one-time saloon queen stalked past Rebecca and thrust open the door to the adjoining room. Rebecca sat down on the bed, engulfed by the hopelessness of it all, yet strangely buoyed up by Honey Anne's surprising outburst.

The front door scraped open.

Rebecca looked up in the half-light of the spluttering lamp. Jeb Ryan's face wore a broad grin, and he reeked of alcohol.

Rebecca glanced away from him.

'You're early,' she said tonelessly.

'There was a bit of an upset at the campfire,' Jeb explained. The girl turned to look at him. 'We were fooling around with the liquor and some spilled on my shirt. Reckon you can wash it out and hang it up so's it'll be dry in the morning.'

Ryan began to shrug out of the shirt and Rebecca saw the flabby flesh of his chest and belly. Hair was matted across his chest and folds of skin dropped over his belt. Suddenly, she felt revulsion and turned her face away. Ryan tossed the liquor-soaked shirt onto her lap, and in that moment all Rebecca's pent-up hatred and scorn boiled to the surface.

She erupted to her feet, lifted the reeking shirt high and threw it back at Jeb Ryan. The garment slapped him wetly across the face and then slithered down his body to the floor. Shaking with rage and fear, Rebecca watched him as his lips parted in a cold smile.

'Know something?' he whispered. 'I kinda like my women to have spirit. However, Rebecca, I also like my women to be obedient. Seems like I'll have to teach you a little lesson.'

Rebecca's eyes never left his as he advanced slowly and deliberately across the room. The lantern glow slanted across his stubbled face and Rebecca saw his eyes narrow as he towered over her.

'Yes, Rebecca,' he purred. 'Reckon you need a lesson – just to let you know where you stand.'

His open hand smashed into her face and with a sharp cry of pain, Rebecca fell backwards. She crumpled into the blankets of the bed as the blood rushed to her cheek. Ruthlessly, Ryan hauled her up, heaving her off the bed. She pummeled his chest with her fists but the outlaw merely laughed and slapped her twice on the face. Rebecca gasped in anguish, flopping down on to the bed again and burying her throbbing face in the blankets. Ryan took one pace and stood motionless beside her. She held her breath, half expecting more punishment, but instead, his claw-like fingers stroked her hair.

'And after you've done that little chore for me,' the outlaw went on, 'you can pretty yourself up for later on. I won't be that late tonight.'

She shivered at his touch.

Ryan stalked out of the room, leaving her alone. Wearily, she walked over to the shirt and picked it up. Her face still stung from Ryan's slaps. That pain would pass. In time, she would become obedient, resigned to her new role. But something would never change as far as Rebecca Donnell was concerned – her loathing for two men. One was the cruel, lustful Ryan who'd forced her to give her body over to his pleasure. The other object of her hatred was a man she and her father used to meet every week at church, a man respected by the entire Boulder Bluff community, a man whom Ridge Donnell always spoke highly of, a pillar of the church and the town. His was the face that had been revealed at the hold-up. His was the experience and cunning which master-minded this outfit from his respectable front of a ranch near Boulder Bluff. Soon, they told her, their boss would be riding to the camp to prepare for the next raid, and once again she would come face-to-face with Pete Kenning, her father's friend and neighbor, the upstanding community man who was in reality the cold, calculating killer known as Long Knife!

They were like ghosts at sundown.

They came up from the narrow pass which joined Black Goose Canyon to the mesa in a long, spectral file, and when they reached the crest, their silhouettes were stark against the crimson veins that made a web across the western skies.

These were no ordinary desert travelers. There was a strangely regimented appearance about their long line, but they weren't soldiers.

Some, however, wore military garb – cavalry shirts, blue pants, army hats. Others were dressed in rags or deerskin britches and some had donned fringed buckskin shirts. They moved with stealth, men who knew every hollow and rock in the desert because they were creatures of the place. Some were half-breeds, strange spawn of white men-Indian squaw couplings; a few were quarter breeds; at least half a dozen were white men, deserters, outcasts from society who'd chosen to ride with this ragged band of renegades.

At their head was a towering figure of a man with a face tanned like leather. Most of the outfit rode wiry ponies, but this man was astride a huge roan gelding. Tall, aloof, Trauba combined the physique of a white frontiersman with the cunning of an Indian. For years he'd led this band of killers as its undisputed head.

'Charlie Sun.' Trauba's voice was sharp, guttural.

The half-breed with a blood-soaked shoulder bandage urged his pony alongside Trauba's horse.

'This is where they stopped.' Trauba had reined in beneath a big cedar.

'The men are tired,' Charlie Sun said.

'But there will be no rest,' Trauba assured him bluntly. 'No rest until we find them. By the looks of these tracks, they have Femo – but we will trail them.'

Charlie Sun grimaced. 'You are reading the trail. How far ahead are they?'

Trauba's inscrutable eyes surveyed the tracks. 'A few hours,' the big half-breed said. 'But not long enough for them to escape us. These are the men who killed my son, and for that, they will die.'

Trauba urged his gelding away from the cedar and the bunch of riders moved across the mesa, and soon night enshrouded the silent mesa. A wan moon climbed the black canvas of sky, filtering just enough light over the mesa for the sharp, penetrating eyes of Trauba to discern the tracks.

No one spoke as they rode. The only sound was the muffled thud of unshod hoofs in the cold sand, a steady drumbeat of impending doom.

SIX

THE GHOST FORT

Femo's face was ashen as the three riders reined in at the foot of the slope.

'Señors,' Femo's tone was tinged with fear. 'I have brought you here! Now, please let me go!'

Shane Preston ignored the whimpering half-breed. Instead, his gray eyes moved over the wind-blasted walls that rose sheer against the moon at the head of the rise.

'So this is Long Knife's camp,' he mused. 'Femo, if this is some sorta trick and you're only foolin'. . . .'

'Señor,' Femo said fervently, 'this is his camp!'

'Reckon he ain't bluffing, Shane,' Jonah muttered.

'An old fort,' Shane observed.

'I figure it's Foster's Outpost.' Jonah was recalling military history. 'Hell, it's not been used for twenty years!'

'Señor,' Femo tremblingly confirmed the old gunfighter's memory. 'This was Foster's Outpost.'

Jonah stroked his beard. 'Soldiers were posted here to put down Kiowa uprisings. A helluva lot of good that did! The red devils massacred two troops of them before the army rode out for the last time.'

'And I suppose folks have just about forgotten this fort's here,' Shane Preston said.

'No one wants to remember it,' Jonah Jones shrugged.

Shane turned his back to the captive. 'Jonah,' he murmured, 'I reckon we've finished with this 'breed-boy. Tie him up and make sure he can't holler out.'

Jonah's six-gun poked into Femo's ribs and the man quivered like a leaf. 'Get off your pony,' Jonah ordered.

Leaving his pard to gag the prisoner and lash him to a tree, Shane prodded Snowfire forward. He headed slowly up the steep slope and the sand-plastered, somber walls loomed up to meet him, their crumbling adobe-brick in deep shadow.

Shane reined in and slipped from his horse. The entrance was just up the rise. Once, twin gates had swung on iron posts, but these had long been ripped away, and now only a black gap remained.

He heard a raucous laugh and moments later saw the fire. Glowing embers were being swirled into the night sky and flickering shadows danced around the dark figures that squatted beside the fiery warmth.

Shane heard the stealthy pad of Jonah's boots in the sand.

'Femo's fixed,' the older gunfighter grunted. 'In fact, he won't be going no place in a hurry.'

'Reckon we'll sneak up there and take a closer look-see,' Shane said softly.

Guns were slipped out of holsters.

Together, Shane and Jonah ran up the slope, melting into the shadows by the entrance. The tall gunhawk let his eyes rove over the parade-ground. The fire was right in the center and its glow extended almost to the buildings that formed a wooden square around the dusty yard. There was a corral over on the opposite side, and Shane could see the shapes of horses in the darkness.

One lamp burned in Foster's Outpost, and Shane perceived the square of light behind the hessian curtain. He motioned to Jonah and the old-timer slid alongside him.

'What do you reckon, Shane?'

'She could be in that room with the light burning,' Shane Preston murmured. 'One thing's for sure. She ain't around the fire. All those four are men – and getting liquored up, by the sounds of things.'

'We going in there to find out?'

'I'm going in there,' Shane said. 'You stay here and cover me. If anything goes wrong, shoot to kill.'

Jonah nodded and crouched down in the darkness.

Shane inched to the gatepost, his back scraping against the old rusted hinges. Very slowly, the gunslinger's tall, lean figure eased through the entrance and stood motionless in the darkness. He glanced over at the fire. One of the outlaws was standing up and drinking from a demijohn, while another upbraided him for not getting on with the poker game in progress. Shane let his eyes return to the lamp-lit window. The room was just along from the old store and fronted by a broken porch.

Keeping his back flat to the wall, Shane began to step furtively around towards the side of the store. Suddenly a log fell in the fire and shooting flames sent a crimson glow to the very walls of Foster's Outpost. There was a whicker from the horse corral and Shane stood like a statue. Gradually the glow retreated like an ebbing tide and Shane crept to the side wall of the store.

He halted beside the bullet-scarred wall, peering in through a silted window. The old army store was heaped with discarded bottles, the aftermath of a hundred aimless drinking sprees. Shane inched to the corner of the store and looked down the long, cracked balcony. Huge splits sliced the wooden boards, one post lay smashed in the dust of the parade-ground, and the roof sagged precariously.

Shane's boots made the crumbling boards creak, but the crackle of the fire and the coarse voices of the outlaws drowned the sounds. With his body scraping the store's front wall, Shane headed towards the next room. The sacking curtains fluttered in the slight breeze as the gunfighter came within an arm's length of the window. He looked back at the campfire. The outlaws appeared engrossed in a new hand of poker.

Slowly, Shane's left hand groped through the paneless aperture and found the edge of the hessian. Inch by inch, his fingers drew the curtain aside to a little chink.

The gunslinger turned his back on the outlaws and glanced swiftly through the slit. The wan lantern glow showed him a woman seated on a crude bed. All he could see was her back.

'Rebecca!' Shane's voice was soft, but urgent. 'Rebecca!' She swiveled around on the bed and Shane saw her shocked face.

Rebecca! He had found her.

Before she could speak, Shane's hand widened the

chink and she could see his face more clearly.

'Don't make a sound! I've been sent by your pa! Ridge Donnell sent me!'

Trembling, Rebecca stared at him. Sheer disbelief surrendered to desperate hope and she opened her mouth to speak, but Shane motioned her to remain silent.

'I'm coming inside, Rebecca,' whispered the gun-fighter. 'Just stay right where you are!'

He crept to the door and lifted the latch. He opened it and slipped swiftly inside. Without a word, he shut the door and slid past the bed to the window. He parted the curtain and surveyed the parade ground, noting that the poker game was still in progress. Finally, he turned to face her. He was smiling.

'Who – who are you?' Rebecca's voice was hoarse, but laden with hope.

'No time for introductions, ma'am,' Shane said wryly. 'Your pa hired me and my pard to find you and bring you back. He'll be waiting with your intended, Stobie, at an old mission called Apache Wells – and that's where we're going right now.'

'Thank God!' she murmured.

'Save the thanks for later,' Shane said grimly. 'We'll have plenty of time to talk when we get out of this camp. Now you don't know me, but you're gonna trust me and do exactly like I say. Understand?'

Rebecca nodded mutely. A few seconds ago, she'd been in the depths of despair. Now, wild hope surged through her.

Shane strode to the window. Suddenly he whipped around, gun poised as the door to the adjacent room whined open. Honey Anne stepped in.

'Rebecca, I wonder if you've got—' She broke off with a gasp when she saw Shane standing there.

'Ma'am,' Shane Preston thumbed back the hammer of his six-gun, 'don't make me plug my first female. Now, just stand right where you are and keep your trap shut while we work things out.'

Honey Anne gaped at him, unable to take in the situation.

'Mister,' Rebecca Donnell broke in frantically, 'she doesn't belong to them. Honey Anne's a prisoner like me.'

'What is this?' Honey Anne demanded incredulously, as Shane lowered his gun.

'He's from pa,' Rebecca cried. 'He's come here to take me home!'

She ran over to Shane and her fingers clutched at his arm.

'Mister,' she pleaded, 'we can't leave Honey Anne here. We have to take her with us.'

There wasn't time to argue. Shane hadn't figured

on sneaking out with two women in tow, but he figured he had no choice. Despite the problems in taking Honey Anne along, he couldn't leave her to languish in this hell-hole.

Honey Anne looked bewildered, completely non-plussed by this sudden turn of events. Nevertheless, she had the presence of mind to plead with Shane.

'Please, mister! Please take me with you!'

'In just a moment,' Shane said, 'we'll all walk slowly and quietly out of this room. No one runs. We slip over to the store. My pard's gun will be covering us from the entrance, but I'm not aiming to stir up a gunfight. I just want us to sneak out of this fort all in one piece.'

There was no time for further explanations, no time for answers to the questions frozen on both the prisoners' lips. Shane eased open the front door.

The card game was breaking up in a babble of argument. Jeb Ryan had erupted to his feet and now, with a sneer at the others, he stalked away

'Oh, God!' Rebecca moaned. 'He's coming this way!'

'Rebecca,' Shane snapped, 'sit down on the bed and smile at him when he comes inside – move!'

Quivering, Rebecca Donnell backed to the bed.

Shane shoved Honey Anne behind the door and joined her. They heard the dull thud of Ryan's boots in the dust.

There was a creak as he mounted the wooden verandah, then a long silence. Shane Preston's hand gripped his gun. Then Ryan's big fingers wrenched the open door wider.

'Good to see you waiting for me,' Ryan complimented Rebecca. 'But why ain't you lyin' down?'

The outlaw took one step inside, kicked the door shut with his heel, and the next moment Shane's gun butt smashed like a hammer into the back of his head. Ryan reeled around, then folded and dropped without a murmur into Shane's arms. Shane lowered him to the floor.

'Check the window,' he told Rebecca.

She glided over to the window. 'All three of them are still around the fire.'

Shane opened the door gently and stepped outside into the darkness of the porch. He motioned to Rebecca, and the slim girl joined him. Honey Anne edged out of the room, and Shane led the captives along the length of the balcony. They slipped into the shadows by the store.

'The last stretch ain't gonna be easy,' the tall gunfighter breathed. 'It's open ground between here and the entrance. We keep our backs hard against the wall and edge around nice and slow-like.'

Shane nudged Rebecca and she nodded. She

moved along the side of the store and flattened her back to the adobe wall that surrounded Foster's Outpost.

'You next,' he prompted Honey Anne.

The former saloon queen drew in her breath and obeyed him. Shane waited until both of the captives were creeping furtively along the wall before he made his move.

Then one of the outlaws stood up at the fire.

'All right! All right, Brett!' he conceded, grudgingly. 'So Jeb was entitled to cuss! Hell – just because I dealt one hand a mite speedy!'

'Yeah, from the bottom of the deck. Go fetch him back,' Brett Dayman grunted. 'The cards run better with four of us. Anyways, he's got all night for that fancy woman of his.' Dayman guffawed at his own quip.

'Yeah, Wes,' Rodd Lewis grinned. 'Go and tear Jeb away from her. We need him more'n she does.'

Morrender stalked towards the room that the prisoners had just fled. By now, Rebecca was almost beside Jonah Jones, who'd stepped out of the shadows to meet her, and Honey Anne wasn't far behind.

Over at the room, Morrender shoved open the door with a raucous laugh.

Now, Shane began to lope towards the gateway to

join Jonah and the women, but moments later there came a yell from Morrender.

'Something's up!' Wes Morrender was bawling, and the other outlaws leaped to their feet. 'Jeb's been hit! He's out to it! And the women have gone!'

There was a stunned silence, then one of the outlaws yelled and pointed to the gateway. Hoarse cries echoed out over Foster's Outpost as they saw Rebecca's figure dashing outside and a stranger standing there with gun raised.

There was a concentrated dive for hardware. But it was Shane's gun that thundered first. Wes Morrender, running down from the balcony, caught the slug in the side of his face and pitched forward to crash headlong into the dust. Yelling, the outlaws fled out of the fire glow which made them perfect targets.

'Take the girls to our horses!' Shane called to Jonah above the crash of gunfire. 'I'll be right with you!'

Crouching in the shadows, Shane took careful aim at a groove in the adobe wall which was just above the level of the horses' heads in the corral. His six-gun boomed and the bullet whined over the frightened horses and spun away from the brick. Already spooked, the white-eyed, plunging animals raced from one side of the crude corral to the other. Shane fired again. A huge chestnut reared high. Two terrified animals surged to the far end of the corral, desperately trying to escape the wicked whine of Shane's bullets. Seeing Shane's intent, the outlaws directed their fire at his gun-flashes, but the tall streak was merely an elusive shadow in the night.

Shane's gun spat again, and this time there was a splintery crash as iron hoofs smashed through the wood of the corral fence. The milling horses surged into the breach and thundered across the parade ground.

The gunfighter zigzagged for the gateway, standing aside as the terrified horses flew through the entrance in a swirl of dust.

He dodged out into the desert. A screaming slug ripped flesh from his left arm and blood surged from the wound like a spring. Two more bullets winged past him into the night. He plunged down the slope to where Honey Anne crouched behind Jonah on the old mare's back. Rebecca was waiting beside Snowfire. She was strangely calm.

Two outlaws ran out of the outpost and stood at the top of the slope. Slugs whined wickedly close as the renegades emptied their guns in wild abandon.

Jonah was already urging Tessie into a run when Shane grabbed Rebecca around the waist and swung her high. The girl clung to Snowfire's white mane as the tall gunfighter vaulted into the saddle behind her.

With one arm wrapped around Rebecca's slender waist, Shane grabbed the reins with his free hand and the palomino responded instantly to his touch. Like a streak in the night, Snowfire raced into the wilderness, leaving the two cursing outlaws struggling to reload their guns.

'You fools!'

Pete Kenning had listened to Brett Dayman's garbled account of the debacle and now he towered above them, his face ashen with cold fury.

'I'm warned by Provis about those two gunslingers nosing around,' Kenning said slowly and with deadly deliberation, 'so I decide to ride out to make sure things are OK. And what do I find?'

The man who called himself Long Knife let his eyes roam over the churned-up dust of the parade ground.

The wrecked corral was in shadow, with splintered lengths of timber strewn in the dust. Right along from the corral lay Wes Morrender, not quite dead, but with his life ebbing away. Beside the dying campfire, Jeb Ryan was slowly coming to.

'I find this!' Pete Kenning snarled.

Dayman swallowed.

'And more important than all this,' went on Kenning, repeating what he'd just been told, 'the prisoners have gone, including the woman I ordered to be killed.'

'Jeb kinda fancied her,' Lewis said sheepishly.

Kenning slid out of his saddle. 'You know what this could mean?' he rasped. 'Those two women know about the camp, and about me. And by now, Donnell's two hired guns will know who runs this outfit. Me!'

'Boss,' Dayman said, trying desperately to retrieve the situation, 'they can't be far away – and they rode double. Once we find our horses, we'll ride 'em down fast!'

'Yeah,' Lewis said hoarsely. 'Reckon we'll be burying them all someplace in this desert before sunup.'

'I hope so,' Kenning said softly. 'For all our sakes. Now get out and fetch back those spooked horses.'

'Boss!' Dayman's mouth had dropped open. 'We've got visitors!'

Pete Kenning swiveled around, his right hand instinctively groping for his gun.

'Hell, no!' Lewis warned him. 'Keep your hand away from that gun! It's Trauba's bunch, and I reckon he wants to talk!'

They filled the entrance to Foster's Outpost. Many of them were in shadow but the moonlight was slanting over the big half-breed who now jogged his

101

mount slowly across the parade ground. The outlaws waited in silence as Trauba came closer and more than a dozen of his outfit filtered through the gateway into the fort. By now, Jeb Ryan was scrambling to his feet, his hands clutching his throbbing head.

Trauba halted and focused his cold, haughty eyes on the group of outlaws. The renegade leader was flanked by two of his men, ragged shadows on pinto ponies, and beside them on foot was a whimpering man with ropes hanging from his wrists.

'Long Knife,' Trauba said, 'I believe we have a common enemy. Two men killed my son, the same two men made this poor fool show them the way here.'

One of the 'breeds lashed out at Femo with his foot and the hapless man staggered away to stand alone by the dying fire.

'If men of the desert have a common enemy,' Pete Kenning said, 'they should join forces.'

Trauba nodded in agreement. 'When we arrived here, we found this clumsy one tied to a tree.' Trauba looked at Femo. 'And we found your horses down the slope.'

The 'breed leader signaled to the dark bunch of riders behind him, and two renegades led a string of roped horses across to them.

'I reckon, Trauba,' Pete Kenning said, 'that we'll get along fine. Brett, saddle those horses.'

Dayman grinned. 'Sure thing, boss.'

Trauba remained in the saddle as Dayman paced to the captured horses. The big man was contemplating the shivering Femo, and finally he turned his eyes back to Kenning.

'Long Knife.' There was a tinge of urgency in his voice. 'Look at the snake.'

Pete Kenning angled his body around. It seemed now that every eye was on Femo.

'This man was scared into helping the men who killed my son,' Trauba said slowly. 'For that alone, I should kill him. But because he harmed you by leading those men to your camp, I'm handing him over to you for punishment. He is yours, Long Knife.'

There was a long silence. Femo moistened his lips and his frightened eyes flitted over the dark, expressionless faces of these desert men.

Very slowly, Kenning drew out his gun. He weighed the six-gun in the palm of his hand and deftly thumbed back the hammer. Every man heard the sharp metallic click. Suddenly Femo whipped around to run. He bounded frantically for the broken corral and Kenning raised his gun. There was an explosion and the bullet carved into Femo's back. No one moved as Femo swung around, groped desperately for the sky and then plunged into the dust of the parade ground.

Kenning slid the six-gun back into its holster and turned to face Trauba. There was a strange smile on the half-breed's thick lips.

'Like you said, Long Knife,' Trauba nodded approvingly at Femo's blood-splashed body, 'we'll get along fine.'

SEVEN

BITTER RENDEZVOUS

It was the hour before sunup, the coldest hour in the wilderness, and the moaning wind from the distant ranges swept over the silent ridges and stirred up the red sand.

Shane dropped his cigarette butt and trod it into the softness. 'The horses have rested long enough,' he said. 'Reckon we'll be moving out.'

'How much longer?' Jonah had been talking to the ex-saloon queen, and now he crossed over to Shane.

'I figure the trail's about an hour's ride,' Shane said. 'We're just about off the mesa.'

Jonah drew on his cigarette. 'So we'll be at that mission in a coupla hours.'

'Maybe.' Shane grinned at his pard. 'You seem to be getting on pretty well with Honey Anne.'

Jonah flushed. 'Doggone it! At least she's a mite more presentable than that two-ton Ada!'

Shane took a drink from his canteen. 'I'd go along with that.'

'Anyhow,' Jonah Jones snorted. 'You ain't doin' so bad yourself, Shane.'

'Uh?'

'Donnell's daughter. I've seen the way she looks at you.'

'Rebecca's on her way to meet the man she'll marry,' Shane said tonelessly.

Jonah grinned knowingly at him and Shane screwed the stopper back into the lip of his canteen.

The tall gunfighter moved over to where Rebecca was resting by a bald-faced boulder. She was slumped in the sand, using the rock as a shelter from the biting wind, and looking down at her, Shane felt the stirring of old desires. He saw the cascade of her black hair, the slim, shapely shoulders of her young body, and momentarily she reminded him of Grace, the woman he'd loved and who now lay cold under the clay. Shane Preston swallowed as the memory began to fade and reality claimed him. His wife was dead and

106

the reason he hired out his gun was to hunt down and kill the last of her murderers.

'Shane. . . .' She was looking up at him.

The gunfighter crouched down beside her. There was a makeshift linen bandage around the top of his left arm where the bullet had torn his flesh and passed on through.

'I'm scared, Shane.'

'Of the outlaws catching up with us?'

She shook her head. 'No,' she said softly. 'If that happens, I know what to expect. Either you and Mr Jones will kill them, or they'll kill us. No, I'm scared of something else.'

Shane placed his hand on her bare arm. Her skin was soft and her eyes met his. 'I'm scared of meeting Oliver.'

'Your intended husband?'

'I'm scared of meeting him like this.' She turned her face away.

Shane smiled. 'Now, don't worry, Rebecca. You can brush your hair, pretty yourself up a little.'

'You don't understand,' she said. 'It's not the way I look, but the way I am.'

'Oh?'

'You can guess what those animals did to me, Shane. It – it happened right beside the stage, and then – then when we got to the camp, Ryan claimed me for himself. I was his woman.' Rebecca lifted her tortured eyes to the gunslinger's. 'I had to cook, wash and – and sleep with him. I had no choice.'

She slipped a hand over his.

'I feel unclean. Maybe I am unclean.'

'Rebecca,' Shane said quietly. There was unusual tenderness in his voice. 'Listen to me. There's no reason for you to feel bad in any way. No one's gonna blame you for what happened when the outlaws captured you. No one.'

Rebecca Donnell swallowed. 'It's just that I'd heard it said a man wouldn't want a woman who'd – well, a woman like me. Used up.'

Shane's fingers closed around hers. 'I'm a man,' he said, 'and if you were my bride, I'd sure still want you.'

A soft smile came to her lips. She leaned forward swiftly and pressed her mouth to Shane's cheek. 'Thank you,' she murmured.

The gunfighter stood up, holding out his hands for her. Rebecca gripped them and he hauled her up. Together they walked towards Snowfire, and Shane scowled at the broad grin cracking Jonah's whiskery face. He helped Rebecca onto the palomino's back, then swung into the saddle himself.

'What are you grinning at, you old goat?' Shane demanded good-naturedly. 'Let's ride.'

They headed out from the hollow and twisted around the ancient peaks that rose like ramparts from the desert floor to hem in the mesa. The descent began and Shane led the way down a long, plunging trail that hugged the sides of the pumice needle. Here they were completely cut off from the wind that had lashed across the tableland, and below them, the wilderness of sand and rock was bathed gray by the first fingers of dawn. Suddenly the eastern sky was aglow and the string of clouds was tinged pink, and with sunup came the breath of warmth. By now they were at the foot of the trail and after a glance at the lonely rim behind them, Shane struck out for the main stage trail.

They mounted a long, rising ridge broken by a hundred knife-edged rocks, and it was here that some sixth sense made Shane Preston rein in. He swiveled around in the saddle, and a muffled curse just along the ridge told him that Jonah had spotted them, too. The length of the mesa rim above the winding track was lined with riders.

'Hell!' Jonah whistled. 'Looks like a damn army up there.'

'There's too many for just the Long Knife outfit,' Honey Anne exclaimed.

'Could be two outfits,' Shane said wryly. 'Long Knife's and that other bunch that's after us. Whoever they are, they're too many to stop and argue with.'

He urged Snowfire off the ridge, and glancing back over his shoulder, he saw the riders filing towards the track. The fugitives headed away from the rise, but their horses were carrying double burdens and only Snowfire seemed to run at close to his usual speed. The old mare snorted and grunted as Jonah urged her to greater efforts, but twice Shane had to rein in and wait for Tessie to catch up.

The minutes fled and the fugitives mounted one ridge, only to be faced with another. Once Shane called a halt, and sitting saddle, they tried to catch a glimpse of the riders behind them. All they could see was a distant spiral of dust.

They plunged deeper into the desert, and climbing to the crest of a low ridge, they saw the trail stretched like a ribbon beneath them. Recalling Hunk O'Malley's instructions, Shane turned his horse west and the riders raced for the trail.

Sweat-streaked and stumbling, their mounts reached the stage trail, but Shane knew they could afford no more rest. By now their pursuers must be drawing close. And so they rode the trail, following the rutted stage tracks into the very heart of the wilderness. Here, hardly a tree showed up from the sand, and the only vegetation was the flowering sage

110

that sometimes stretched right over the trail. Still the fugitives rode. Exhausted, Honey Anne simply clung to old Jonah as the dust plastered her hair and got into her eyes. The trail twisted around a gigantic butte, mounted a long, low rise and then dropped to a fork below. One track veered south for Sand Creek, the other west for Sonora, and right in the V of the fork stood the sun-bleached walls of their destination.

Shane felt Rebecca's sigh of relief, and she leaned back against him with a grateful smile.

'We made it,' she whispered.

'We made it here,' Shane agreed. 'But I figure we've bought ourselves a whole heap of trouble.'

'And by now that trouble's not far behind,' Jonah remarked as he thrust an anxious look over his shoulder. 'I'm not getting religion after all these years, but let's get the hell down to that church!'

The gunfighters turned their mounts down the slope, following the well-worn trail into the shadows of the adobe walls that rose tall and sheer into the azure. Looking like a medieval fortress, the mission stood as a silent monument, its big, thick walls lined with tiny barred windows.

Shane reined in beneath the curving Spanish arch and surveyed the closed gate with its hand-carved inscription.

APACHE WELLS MISSION.
MISSIONER: FATHER MATTHEW LOCKLEY.

The pudgy gunslinger frowned at two freshly painted words written beneath the missioner's name.

'Heck! Is that his assistant?'

' "*Adeste Fideles*" is Latin,' Shane Preston grinned. 'Some sorta text.'

'It means 'come in, men of faith',' Honey Anne said, flushing deeply. 'You see, once I went to a convent school – but that was a long time ago.'

Gaping at this display of knowledge, Jonah merely sat back baffled while Shane hammered on the door. They didn't have to sit saddle for long. There was the soft pad of shoes and the jangling of keys, followed by a long silence.

'Who is it?' The voice was oddly cultured.

'Unlock the gate, Father,' Shane called out. 'We're here to meet Oliver Stobie and Mr Donnell.'

'Ah yes!' They heard the metallic click of a key fitting into a lock. 'You are expected.'

'Figured you might have seen us coming,' Shane Preston said as the key turned.

There was a pause. 'I've been in the chapel, my son.'

The gate whined wide and a jovial-faced little priest

smiled a welcome. His hair was cut in a fringe, and looking down from their saddles, the gunfighters saw the tonsured bald patch on the crown of his head.

'Welcome to the mission,' Father Lockley said. 'I presume you'll be Mr Preston and Mr Jones?'

'You – uh – knew we was comin'?' Jonah gulped, his wide eyes glued to the long, flowing cassock Father Lockley wore.

'Mr Stobie is already here,' the priest explained. 'Arrived on the Sand Creek stage one hour ago. He showed me Mr Donnell's letter, truly a letter written by a man of deep faith. I might add, judging by the young ladies you have with you, faith well-founded. I might add again, of course, that since Mr Stobie arrived and I learned of your mission, I did engage in prayer for you both.'

'Thank you, Father,' Shane said politely. 'Now, if it's OK with you, we'll head inside.'

Lockley stood aside as Shane jogged Snowfire under the archway and into the mission courtyard. Jonah came right behind him, breathing a huge sigh of relief as he glanced at the high walls that enclosed them.

'Father,' Shane said. 'I reckon it might be wise for you to lock and bar that gate. There's a big bunch of renegades trailing us.'

'Holy Mother!' The priest crossed himself quickly

and ran back to the gate. Within seconds, he'd locked it and dropped an iron bar over two stout hooks.

Shane glanced around at the mission. Thick walls enclosed a courtyard, a well, and three main buildings. There was a chapel in the far western corner with a slate roof, stained glass windows and a cross carved in the door. Just along from this place of worship was a long, wide building that looked like a schoolhouse, and tucked beneath the eastern wall, a small log cabin. A balcony ran right around the walls.

The tall gunfighter slipped out of the saddle.

He held out his arms for Rebecca. He felt her tremble as he lifted her down, and momentarily, their bodies were touching.

'I reckon,' Shane said as the diminutive priest came running up, 'Rebecca would like to see her fiancé.'

'Of course, of course,' Father Matthew Lockley smiled. 'I'll awaken him.'

'You mean Stobie's asleep?' Jonah demanded as he dismounted.

'Mr Stobie had a long, arduous ride in that stage from Sonora,' Lockley shrugged. 'So I told him to lie down in the rest-room.'

'Rebecca's had an arduous ride, too,' Shane said bluntly. 'Go wake him up.'

Father Matthew Lockley nodded and walked over

to the log cabin. By now, Honey Anne had swung out of the saddle and stood in the center of the yard, brushing the dust from her clothes. Lockley shoved open the cabin door.

'Mr Stobie!' The priest's voice echoed hollowly.

A few seconds later, Lockley emerged and waited by the door. There was a dull thud of boots and finally Stobie swayed outside and surveyed them in the warmth of the morning sun. At first Oliver Stobie said nothing. He simply stood there, blinking sleepily, a slim man dressed in a hand-tailored suit and white silken shirt, clothes which looked as incongruous as the priest's full length cassock in the desert.

Rebecca whispered his name, but still he didn't move.

Then she went towards him, slowly at first, but suddenly breaking into a run. Reaching him, Rebecca threw her arms around his neck, pressing her softness against him. She searched frantically for his mouth, finding it and molding her lips to his. For a long moment they clung to each other.

'Oliver!' she murmured as he kissed her briefly on the cheek. 'Oh, my darling!'

He held her then, allowing Rebecca to clutch him, but all at once he pushed her away and Shane exclaimed:

'Heck, we're embarrassin' this young couple,

gawkin' at them this way! Say, Father, how about rustling up some grub for us?'

'Of course, of course,' the priest agreed. 'Follow me.'

'Wait, please,' Rebecca Donnell called out. 'I want Oliver to meet you all. Oliver, these are my friends. Shane and Jonah rescued me from the outlaws.'

'Outlaws?' Stobie gasped.

'The stage wasn't just lost, Oliver,' she explained. 'Outlaws held it up, killed the men, and – and took me back to their camp. It was there I met Honey Anne.'

The former saloon queen smiled at him.

Stobie forced a smile in return. 'Thank you, gentlemen. I believe Mr Donnell will be paying you well.'

And with that brief comment, Oliver Stobie ushered his bride-to-be into the cabin.

Shane stood there for a moment, thinking, as the door was firmly shut, then he followed Jonah, Honey Anne and the black-frocked missioner into the long hall.

I want you to tell me what happened, Rebecca,' Oliver Stobie said. He was wide awake now, his eyes wary.

She was seated on the bunk while her fiancé stood against the log wall, twirling an unlit cigarillo.

Stobie's face was pallid, more so than hers, and his fingers were agitated. From the first moment they'd entered the cabin, his eyes hadn't left her, and now once again they roved over her, almost appraising her. They took in the torn bodice of her dress, the strands of loose cotton where once buttons had been sewn, and finally they lifted to her wan, tortured eyes.

'What do you mean?' she breathed. 'I told you. The outlaws held up the stage and killed everyone. . . .'

'Rebecca,' he cut in, 'you told me all that. I want to know what else happened – at the camp.'

She swallowed. 'You mean, how they treated me?'

'You know what I mean.' There was more than a hint of censure in his tone. Abruptly, the semblance of warmth he'd displayed in the courtyard had vanished and there was coldness in his voice. 'Tell me exactly what happened, Rebecca.'

Tears sprang to her eyes.

'Oliver,' she pleaded, 'I want to forget what happened. Please – please just hold me, accept me! We can talk about other things later.'

She rose from the bunk and moved towards him, but Stobie made no attempt to reach out for her. In fact, he actually took two steps away from her and stared at the other wall.

'What is it?' But she already knew the answer.

He lit his cigarillo and blew out the flaming vesta. 'Know something, Rebecca?' Stobie said, and she closed her eyes. 'Know what I always dreamed of? A good home, an honest job, and a woman pure and untainted standing beside me in front of the preacher. Remember how I used to talk about those things? Remember what it meant to me?'

Rebecca nodded, the cold hand of dread clutching at her heart. The purity of the woman he married had always been a favorite subject of his. At the time, she'd taken little notice of his fanaticism. After all, what was there to debate? She had never given herself to a man.

'Yes, Oliver,' she said meekly.

'Well?' he demanded.

She looked imploringly up at him, hoping, praying that he would put an end to this terrible questioning, but Stobie was like a man possessed. The veins stood out on his temples, and she knew he would nag at her until he got the truth.

'Before I tell you what happened, Oliver,' she said quietly, 'just answer me one question. Do you love me?'

'Rebecca!' His voice was hoarse. 'I've a right to know what happened.'

And suddenly she was seeing Oliver Stobie as she'd never seen him before. Gone was the facade of charm

118

and polish. Gone was the dandy dresser who'd wooed and won her, the man she'd learned to respect. In his place was the real Oliver Stobie, whose love for her was conditional upon her so-called purity.

'All right,' Rebecca breathed. 'If you want to hear it, then I'll tell you just what happened. The outlaws held up the stage, killed all the men, shot them down in cold blood. They were going to do the same to me, but they decided on something else.'

Stobie's face was ashen as he dragged on his cigarillo.

'They – they misused me, Oliver.' She looked him straight in the eyes. 'And then they took me back to their camp and made me an outlaw's woman. I belonged to Jeb Ryan. I had no choice, Oliver. I was forced to be his woman.'

Stobie stared at her. 'You gave yourself to him?'

'No,' Rebecca shook her head. 'He took me.'

There was a long, terrible silence. Stobie took the cigarillo from his lips and flicked the ash over the floor.

'In your eyes,' she said softly and deliberately, 'what happened makes me unclean.'

He looked at her. She hadn't asked a question; merely stated a fact.

'I reckon we'll go and join the others,' Oliver Stobie said, his voice toneless. He unlatched the door.

It swung open and let in the hot sunlight, but all Rebecca Donnell felt was coldness. Stobie didn't even look back. He walked out to the courtyard, leaving her alone in her shattered world.

Suddenly there was a hoarse cry of warning.

Rebecca dashed away her tears and went to the door. Shane Preston was loping across the yard, making for the ladder which led to the parapet and the top of the wall. Stobie stood stunned, then yelled a question which Shane ignored as he scaled the ladder. Running in Shane's wake was Father Lockley, his cassock billowing out like a black sail, and behind him, a puffing, red-faced Jonah brandishing a long Winchester. Shane was on a parapet now and peering out over the top of the wall.

Rebecca glanced up at the sky. Dust hung in the azure blue. Dust whipped up by pounding hoofs.

Seconds later, Shane confirmed all their fears. He turned around as they gathered at the foot of the ladder and his tone was terse.

'They're on the ridge,' he said. 'About twenty of them.' Father Matthew Lockley crossed himself.

EIGHT

DEAL WITH THE DEVIL

Shane waited as Father Lockley and Jonah clambered up the ladder and ran along the parapet. Breathlessly, the little priest came alongside him, and looked out cautiously. At last he said, 'Just like the days of the Apache uprising!' The priest surveyed the line of riders on the ridge overlooking the mission. 'They came like ghosts out of the desert, killed two priests and desecrated the chapel. That's when the mission was closed.'

'Closed?' Shane kept his eyes firmly fixed on the riders.

'Only I remained, and I told my superiors I would be staying on,' Matthew Lockley said. 'Regardless of the heathen, the Lord sent me here, and I wasn't going to ride out to safety. This mission contains a chapel and a school and a rest-room for weary travelers, and it needs someone to look after it.'

'Know something?' Shane mused. 'Those renegades out there won't be too sure how many of us are inside. They know there are four of us and they've probably heard you're the only priest, Father. What they won't be sure of is how many travelers or other folks you have here.'

Lockley smiled. 'That's true! At times there have been over a dozen folks taking refuge here.'

Shane watched as three of the riders bunched together, while the others stayed in a line.

'Those riders are desert men,' Shane said. 'They'd know about this mission and the travelers who stop over here. I reckon that right now they're debating just how many they have to face.'

'Maybe,' Jonah growled at his pard, 'we ought to try and convince 'em the odds are stacked against 'em.'

'Just what I was figuring, Jonah,' Shane Preston said slowly. He turned to Father Lockley. 'There are rifles and spare six-guns on our horses. Get the women and Stobie up here with those guns. We're gonna make it sound like there's a small army in here.'

'Wouldn't it sound even more impressive if each person was firing two guns at once?' Lockley asked.

'Sure would,' Shane Preston said. 'But Stobie didn't look like he was carrying a gun, and we haven't enough for each person to have two.'

Father Matthew Lockley grinned. 'Follow me.'

Shane shrugged and turned to Jonah. 'Keep watch!'

The priest was already climbing down the ladder and the gunfighter took a last glance at the outlaws before striding after him. He slid down the ladder two rungs at a time and joined Lockley on the ground.

'Let me explain something, Mr Preston,' Father Lockley said, as they walked together across the court-yard. 'I'm an ordained priest, a man of God. I'm also a man of trust, a man of the Good Book. I'm against violence.'

'Yeah.'

Lockley guided the gunfighter around the side of the hall and paused beside the wall. Kneeling down, he began to scrape away the sand from a spot below a window, and watching intently, Shane saw a wooden trapdoor slowly revealed. The priest shoveled away the last handfuls of sand and stood up.

'I said I was against violence,' the missioner said. 'But I also recall how my brother priests were butchered and God's house broken into. I, too, would have been killed if it hadn't been for the arrival of a relief column. Ever since, I've been prepared for an emergency.'

He crouched down and his hand fastened around an iron ring. He heaved the trapdoor open and a musty smell came up. Shane squinted down into the darkness. There was a ladder leading into the cellar, and the priest grinned at his companion before starting to climb through the square hole.

Shane lowered his body after him. Swiftly, he joined the priest on the soft, damp earth.

The cellar was as small as a prison, a tiny square sanctuary carved out of the ground. Its walls were wet, mossy and crumbling, and the floor was earthen. A shaft of light from the open trapdoor played over two neatly stacked boxes and three water-canteens.

Lockley unlatched the first box and pulled the lid back. Shane smiled as the light fell on a pile of army carbines and ammunition containers.

'An emergency?' Shane raised his eyebrows.

'I grabbed these from the dead Apaches after the soldiers opened fire on them,' Father Matthew Lockley said unblushingly.

'And the cartridges?'

'Er – bought from the gunsmith in Sonora,' Lockley murmured.

'What's in the other box?'

'Take a look-see yourself,' the priest invited.

Shane lifted the rifle box to the ground and prised open the lid of the second one. The smell of gunpowder rose to his nostrils.

'Figured it might come in handy,' the missioner said.

Shane closed the lid of the gunpowder container and grabbed half a dozen carbines.

'Bring some of those cartridges, Father,' Shane said.

The gunfighter climbed up the ladder while Lockley rummaged in the box. Once out in the sun, Shane waited for the priest. Finally Father Lockley emerged from the cellar, the pockets of his black cassock bulging with ammunition. Lockley kicked the trap-door back into place and scraped sand over the wood with his boot.

Then the gunfighter and the priest walked together across the courtyard.

Briefly, Shane explained his scheme to Stobie and the two women.

'You had no right to bring these outlaws here!' Stobie stammered. 'You should have shaken them off your trail before making for the mission. Hell, man, you've endangered all our lives, including this ordained priest's!'

Shane felt anger boil up within him. 'It so happens, Stobie,' the gunfighter said coldly, 'it was your bride-to-be we brought here. There was no time to cover our trail, and it was either ride straight here or face them in the desert. If we'd stopped, Rebecca would be dead by now.'

'You made the right decision,' Father Lockley told Shane. 'After all, this mission was built as a sanctuary.'

Shane shoved a carbine into Stobie's hands.

'See here!' Stobie blustered. 'This – this is an army carbine. I've never fired one before. Absolutely never! I just wouldn't know how.'

'As good a time as any to learn,' Shane Preston remarked wryly. 'Now I suggest you get up on that wall and ask Jonah for a quick lesson.'

Still protesting volubly, Oliver Stobie was shoved towards the ladder.

'How about you, Honey Anne?' Shane asked.

The ex-saloon queen grabbed two carbines and held them aloft with a flourish. 'I'll soon work out how to use 'em.'

Shane handed two guns to the priest who promptly bore them to the foot of the ladder. Running over to their horses, Shane unsheathed their rifles and whipped the spare six-guns out of the saddlebags. Together with Rebecca, he paced over to the ladder. They climbed up and joined the other defenders on the wall. The quivering Stobie was being lectured by old Jonah, but the priest alongside him was loading his guns like a seasoned campaigner. Shane glanced towards the ridge. The line of riders had broken up, and most of them were milling around a core of three men who were still talking.

'All right,' Shane said, looking along the row of men and women who stood ready with loaded guns, 'we now convince those renegades out there that we've a damn platoon of soldiers in here! Open fire!'

Six guns blasted the desert silence, and a deadly fusillade of flying lead splattered the crest of the ridge. One 'breed flung up his ragged arms as a slug burned into his chest, and his hoarse cry rang out above the gunshot echoes before he plunged to the desert sand. One pony reared in terror with a bullet embedded in its flanks, tossing its rider aside like a wet sack. Yet another 'breed began to charge down the slope and Shane picked him off with his second shot, lifting him from his pony and plastering him into the dust. All along the walls, guns were thundering in a wild, erratic symphony. Most of the defenders were using two guns at different intervals and Shane was running and firing, changing his position continually.

Shane heard Jonah cursing and then the old-timer stooped down to reload. The priest was keeping up with them. His two carbines ran out of ammunition, and muttering a word which made Jonah gape, Father Lockley fumbled to reload. Shane stood up and his guns blasted again. By now the riders were scattering, streaming further along the ridge or melting behind the crest. Just along the wall, Honey Anne was firing shot after shot at them, while Rebecca fought to level her carbine once again. After firing three bullets, Stobie simply stood there, pale as a ghost, his carbine hanging from a drooping hand.

'Hold it!' Shane called out. 'I reckon that's enough to convince them there are enough of us here who mean business!'

The renegades were in complete disarray, scattered all over the ridge with their ponies running wild and free. Only the Long Knife outfit remained intact, and Shane saw the four outlaw riders disappearing over the ridge.

'Jonah,' Shane said, 'watch them and keep out of sight. We'll all climb down into the yard. That way, they won't be able to count us and we'll keep 'em guessing.'

Stobie for one, needed no second prompting. He ran for the head of the ladder and almost leaped down the rungs. Honey Anne followed him, and the missioner went next. Shane climbed down, waiting on the ground to assist Rebecca. She took his hand and he steadied her as she stepped to the ground.

Shane looked around for Stobie, but he was stalking for the log cabin.

He hardly needed to ask her a question for he could read the misery in her eyes. In fact, it was Rebecca who volunteered the answer.

'Shane,' she whispered. 'I was right. In Oliver's eyes I'm tainted.'

'You stay here, Rebecca,' the gunslinger told her. 'I've a few words to say to Mr Stobie!'

'Please don't!' she pleaded. 'It won't do any good!'

But Shane was already striding across the yard. He cast a long shadow and his steps were firm and straight, and as he walked, the fury inside him mounted to a peak. He thrust open the door and Stobie scowled at him and snapped, 'Preston, if you think I'm going to stand up there again, then think again. You have no authority to order me around.'

'For all the good you did up there on the wall, you might as well have stayed here,' Shane said bluntly. 'No, Stobie. I'm here to talk about something else.'

'Oh?'

Shane kicked the door shut. 'About you and Rebecca.'

Stobie stared at him. 'Don't poke your nose into business that isn't yours, Preston.'

'I'm making it my business!' Shane grated. 'Let me tell you something about yourself, Stobie. You're nothing but a self-righteous son of a bitch, and yellow at that.'

'Listen, Preston – '

'You listen! Rebecca's been through one helluva

129

ordeal. Those animals forced her to submit to them. She was made to do what she did, made to degrade herself. She did nothing to be ashamed of. Nothing, Stobie. And you ought to love her enough and be man enough to accept her. Know what she needs from you now? She needs love!'

A sneer crossed Stobie's face. 'You seem real anxious to help Rebecca with her problems, don't you, Preston? In fact, I'm beginning to wonder what the hell's your stake in this.'

'Spell out what you mean, Stobie,' the tall gunfighter said quietly.

'Did she oblige you back on the trail – like she did those outlaws?' The instant he said it, he knew he'd made a mistake.

Shane's iron fist slammed like a hammer into Stobie's mouth. With a choking cry, the dandy crashed back and rocked into the wall. The gunslinger waded into him, ripping two punches into his chest. Stobie spun away, kicking and clawing wildly as Shane bored relentlessly into him and punched him onto the bunk. The dandy scrambled to his feet and this time Shane blackened his right eye with a searing blow. Stobie wheeled around, aimed a harmless punch at Shane's chest and then caught all the gunslinger's pent-up fury in three bone jarring blows that sent him crashing backwards. The back of his head hit the window, shattering

130

the pane into flying fragments, and the next moment the door was thrown open.

'Holy Mother!' Lockley exclaimed as the bloodied Stobie lunged past him and fled into the courtyard.

'He sure asked for it, Father,' Shane said bluntly. 'In fact, he was damn lucky I didn't kill him.'

'Maybe you're right.' There was a troubled look in Father Matthew Lockley's eye. 'But I think you've more dangerous enemies outside the walls.'

Shane gave the missioner a look, then nodded.

'Guess he riled me some. But he had it comin'.'

The sun was well past its zenith, and already its slow slant to the western rims had started. The brazen heat of midday had long surrendered to the drowsy warmth of afternoon.

It had been a day of waiting for the attack which never came.

Standing in the shadows of the archway, Stobie watched as Father Lockley climbed the ladder to replace Shane on the wall. In an hour's time it would be his turn, but Oliver Stobie wasn't planning to be around to take his rostered duty.

He stepped further back under the arch, flattening himself to the huge entrance gate as Shane exchanged words with the priest and then started to walk towards the head of the ladder.

Cold sweat broke out on Stobie's brow. He'd come all this way to collect his bride, but instead he'd been presented with a woman who'd shared a bed with a common outlaw. Furthermore, he'd been placed in the same peril as the rest of them, and seeing the numbers outside, he'd had few illusions about the ultimate fate of the defenders of Apache Wells. Maybe that initial fusillade had baffled the renegades, but it was only a matter of time before they'd be swarming down the slope to overwhelm the fugitives inside the mission. Donnell would probably be riding up soon, perhaps even with some of his rangeriders, but the outlaws and half-breeds would still have enough numbers to destroy them all.

And Oliver Stobie had no intention of dying with the rest of them.

His body still throbbed from the beating Shane Preston had handed out to him. He waited, motionless, his hate-filled eyes following the tall man as Shane headed for the wall. Only then did Stobie turn his back on the yard. He lifted the iron bar from its hooks.

He fumbled in his pocket and drew out the key-ring he'd just taken from the chapel porch. Earlier, he'd seen Father Lockley hang the ring there, and it had been a simple matter to slip into the church entrance and steal the keys.

Shaking, he chose the longest key, the one which

fitted the big lock. He slid the key deep into the hole and slowly turned it. There was a sharp click. The sweat was running down over his cheeks as he slowly edged the gate open. He pulled the gate wider still and raised his eyes to the crest. The afternoon sun bathed the silent watchers on the ridge.

Stobie paused, as if contemplating the gamble he had decided to take. He glanced back at the mission courtyard. Here, there could be only death. Outside, he had a chance for life.

Wiping the sweat from his brow, he stepped out into the desert.

He began to walk, slowly at first, then stumbling quickly up the slope. There was a yell from one of the half-breeds and Stobie desperately waved his white handkerchief as he ran towards the crest. Behind him, Father Lockley bellowed out a frantic warning, but Stobie paid no heed. He ran faster, his boots sliding in the soft sand. Suddenly two riders headed his way and Stobie stood stock-still with his white 'kerchief fluttering from his outstretched hand.

The two 'breeds rode right up to him and Stobie stared at the naked muzzles of their guns. One of them leaned over on his pinto pony and jabbed his rifle right into Stobie's temple. Oliver Stobie froze and the 'kerchief was blown from his hand.

'I come as a friend,' gasped Stobie. 'You can put

away those guns.'

'Walk!' the 'breed repeated.

Riders flanked him as he climbed the slope. He passed groups of renegades, turning his face away from their cold stares. The wind began to rise, ruffling out the silken fabric of his shirt. Stobie reached the crest and four riders rose seemingly out of the desert itself to confront him. Three of them were white men, and he guessed they must be the dreaded Long Knife outfit. The other rider who reined in his horse and towered over Stobie could only be the legendary Trauba.

'You came with a white flag,' Trauba stated in his deep voice.

'I came to make a deal!' Stobie looked past the half-breed at the trio of outlaws. 'It's a deal I'm offering!'

'You're making a deal on behalf of all those in Apache Wells?' Kenning was rolling a cigarette.

'No.' Stobie shook his head desperately. 'A deal on behalf of myself.'

'Talk!' Trauba said.

'Listen, all of you!' Oliver Stobie was quivering. 'This fight you have with those men isn't mine. Count me out!'

'The deal,' Trauba reminded him coldly.

Stobie swallowed. 'I'm here to offer you two things, for a horse and a safe ride out.'

'What things?' Jeb Ryan growled.

'Information, for one,' Stobie stammered. 'I reckon you'd want to know just how many are behind those walls. When they blasted at you earlier on, you probably figured it was almost an army in there.'

The outlaws exchanged glances but Trauba's face was as expressionless as chiseled rock.

'I'll tell you how many's there,' the dandy said. 'Three men and two women. Just five in all. That shooting from the wall was all a big show to fool you. Now, if you want to take the mission, I suggest you act pronto. A rancher named Donnell is due soon and he'll be bringing riders with him.'

Kenning dragged on his cigarette. 'That was the information. What's the second thing?'

Stobie put his hand into his hip pocket and pulled out a brown leather wallet.

'Money,' he said. 'Currency bills.'

Trauba appeared unmoved, but the outlaws slid out of their saddles as Stobie opened up his wallet. Greedy eyes watched as he ran his fingers over the bills. Ryan strode over to him and held out his hand. There was a confident smile on Oliver Stobie's face as he placed the wallet in the outlaw's gnarled palm. Jeb started counting.

There was a long, pregnant silence during which Stobie stuck his fingers in the lapels of his jacket.

'Is it a deal?' he demanded confidently.

Long Knife shrugged. 'It ain't for me to say.'

'What do you mean?'

'Trauba's boys escorted you up here, so I reckon that makes you his prisoner. Up to Trauba.'

'No! It's up to you!' Stobie croaked frantically.

Kenning shook his head. 'You came up here talking about a deal and the way you wanted things to be. OK, so you've shown your cards.'

The cold hand of terror seized the dandy as he looked from the grinning outlaws to the dark, brooding eyes of Trauba. Now he knew he'd been over-confident and had outbidden his hand.

'He's all yours, Trauba,' Kenning said.

Trauba raised a hand and immediately three riders converged on the whimpering turncoat. Too terrified to run, Stobie stood, shaking, as the 'breeds slithered from their ponies and surrounded him.

'You know something?' Trauba said. 'I'd have treated you better if I'd captured you fighting. At least I would have captured a man.'

Grimy hands grabbed him.

'There's a big ant-hill down from the ridge,' Trauba said simply. 'Use it.'

Stobie screamed, falling limp as the 'breeds began to drag him down from the crest behind the ridge.

'So long, Judas,' said Kenning and shrugged.

NINE

GUNS AT APACHE WELLS

They could hear his screams from the wall, long and piercing and echoing out over the desert. Standing beside Shane, Rebecca was white-faced but tearless as she realized what was happening to the man she'd once planned to marry.

It was Jonah who gave voice to what they all knew to be true. 'Hunk told me about Trauba,' he said hoarsely. 'He likes ant-hills. Hell, Shane, we can't just stand here and listen and do nothin'!'

'Got no choice,' Shane told him bluntly. 'Trauba would just love to have us ride out and try a fool rescue stunt. We'd be cut down in seconds. No, Stobie made his choice to desert us. Now he'll have to pay.'

'And it looks like Stobie talked, too,' Father Matthew Lockley stated, his fingers clenched white over his gun. 'Just as well we closed the gate. They're getting ready to attack.'

Shane picked up his Winchester. 'Father,' he said, 'you stay right here on this wall with the women. Wait till they ride up real close and make every bullet count. Me and Jonah will stake out on the front wall over the arch.'

The gunfighters strode along the parapet, heading swiftly for the point where the wall topped the Spanish arch.

Shane crouched low and checked his rifle. He raised his steely eyes to the ridge where the half-breeds were gathering for the onslaught. He could hear their shouting, could see the big 'breed who was calling them all into line. Just up on the crest, the group of white outlaws sat waiting.

'I guess this is it,' Jonah said soberly, mopping his brow. He sounded calm because he felt that way. Fighting was his trade.

The renegades surged down the slope in a ragged line. Shane and Jonah leveled their rifles together, fingers on triggers. The line swooped closer and some of the renegades were shooting haphazardly. A bullet thudded into the adobe brick of the Spanish arch. Another whined close to Jonah's ears and the oldster let out a well-chosen curse. Shooting broke out from the other wall, and glancing around, Shane saw the priest pumping shot after shot into the oncoming renegades. One of Trauba's men plunged dead to the sand, another slumped forward over his horse's neck, and then the two gunfighters joined in. Flying lead raked from the walls and answering fire splattered around the defenders.

Like vultures, the half-breeds swooped, swarming up to the very walls and pouring lead up at the fugitives. Shane's gun belched time and time again. Beside him, Jonah aimed at a thin half-breed, but the raider's gun thundered first, and the gunhawk swore as the bullet slashed through the top of his shoulder. Jonah dropped his rifle and his claw-like fingers tried to stem the blood flowing from his wound.

Shane stooped, grabbed the oldster's rifle and emptied it at a bunch of 'breeds now milling at the foot of the slope and blasting at the mission's gate.

Still the 'breeds rode closer and Shane killed one as rifle bullets slashed at the wood around the gate's hinges. Crouched on the wall, Shane could hear the dull thuds of slugs striking home. Beneath him, the archway gate was shuddering under a dozen impacts.

The 'breeds slipped from their horses, and Jonah, ignoring the blood streaming from his shoulder, took up his gun again. Side by side, the gunfighters poured lead down into the swirling dust and suddenly the shooting died as the 'breeds retreated back up the slope. The dust settled. Four ragged bodies lay in the sand below the wall. One pony, mortally wounded, was trying vainly to scramble up from the dust. Splinters of wood lay over the churned-up sand in front of the gate.

'Shane!' It was Father Lockley's voice.

The gunfighter loped back along the parapet.

The defenders had paid a terrible price for repelling that first attack. Shane drew in his breath as he saw the crumpled body of Honey Anne. The ex-saloon queen was sprawled over the platform, a bullet in her head. She was still clutching the army carbine in her clenched right hand. Beside her, slumped against the wall was Rebecca, and as Shane stooped down, he saw the small rip in the top of her blood-soaked dress. He glanced up at the priest. Father Lockley's cassock was powder-burnt and torn but he appeared to be unhurt.

Shane drew out his long knife and sliced back the top of Rebecca's dress. Her hand gripped his arm as he wiped away the blood with his 'kerchief. There was a hole right in the center of her shoulder and he could see the dark, ugly outline of the embedded bullet.

'It's not in far.' he said softly, 'You probably caught a ricochet from the top of the wall.'

'I'll – I'll be OK,' she winced.

'If there's time I'll slice it out,' Shane told her.

Father Lockley was climbing down the ladder.

'I think we ought to take a look at that gate,' he said.

Leaving Jonah with Rebecca, Shane descended the ladder and joined the missioner as he strode across the yard. The grayness of oncoming evening was starting to spread over the desert and the sun was a crimson ball above the western rims. The gunhawk and the priest cast long shadows as they stood in front of the gate.

'Just about shot off its hinges,' Father Lockley said ruefully. 'I reckon that they'll blast the gate right down when they come the next time.'

'Which I figure will be in around half an hour,' Shane Preston told him. 'At sundown.'

Lockley ran his hand over the iron bar. Once the gate was blown in, only this bar stood between the renegades and the mission courtyard.

'There's a few of 'em dead out there,' Shane said. 'That's why I figure they'll only come when it's close to dark. It'll be harder for us to pick them off.'

141

Lockley crossed himself. 'And like I said, next time they'll sure blast this gate down! They'll ride right inside!'

'Know something, Father?' Shane said. 'If they're gonna come in, then maybe we ought to arrange a little welcome inside the walls.'

'Huh?'

'First, though, we'll take Rebecca to safety and Jonah can look after her. Then you and me can arrange that house-warmin' for our friends.'

A shadow passed over them, and looking up sharply, they glimpsed the dark silhouette of a buzzard as it swooped past the mission in the dying sunlight.

'Shane,' Father Lockley confessed in a whisper. 'There's something I have to tell you. I'm damn scared.'

Shane held the bullet between his thumb and forefinger. 'How's Jonah?' Rebecca asked the gunfighter.

Shane dropped the spent slug into the pan of hot water. 'He got it just about the same place as you, only his bullet passed right on through. He'll be OK. That pard of mine's as tough as a durn buffalo.'

Rebecca forced a smile. She watched intently as he wrapped the clean linen bandage around her bare shoulder. The top of her dress had been cut right away and folded over the swell of her breasts, and

Shane's hand moved deftly and carefully to avoid hurting her.

'Shane,' she said softly. 'It was so terrible, so humiliating with Oliver! You know, after he finished talking to me, I actually began to feel unclean!'

The gunhawk picked up the knife he'd scarified before using it to cut out the slug. He slipped the blade back into its sheath. Next he corked the iodine and placed the pan back on the table.

'And now?' Shane asked her.

She looked hard at him from the bunk she was lying on. 'Remember back on the trail?' she murmured. 'Remember what you said?'

Shane sat down on the bunk.

'You said that if I was your bride-to-be, you'd still want me in spite of what had happened to me,' she reminded him.

She reached out and inched a soft hand along his arm.

'I recall saying that,' admitted the gunfighter.

'Did you mean it, Shane?'

He bent over and fastened his mouth over hers. He heard a little sob deep in her throat and then her lips parted under his. He kissed her gently and then drew away.

'Know something?' she said with a smile. 'I feel clean again.'

There was the thud of boots at the entrance to the hall. Jonah ambled inside and grinned knowingly as Shane stood up from the bunk. 'Reporting for duty!' he said, holding his rifle aloft.

'Look after Rebecca,' Shane told him. 'The priest and I have some work to do. When the chore's done, I want you to take Rebecca to the cellar and stay with her.'

Shane started to stride away.

'Shane!' Rebecca called out after him. He paused at the door. 'Shane,' she said sincerely. 'Thank you.'

He walked out into the gathering dusk, heading towards the lonely figure on the wall. He mounted the ladder and Father Lockley turned as he came alongside.

By now the crimson sundown was bathing the rims and its dying light stretched out to finger the ridge overlooking Apache Wells Mission. Sprawled bodies lay cold in the sand where they'd fallen, but on the crest, men and horses were stirring.

'Everything ready for that welcomin' party?' Shane Preston wanted to know.

'Just about,' the missioner nodded. 'The box of black powder has been taken out of the cellar. Now all we have to do is bury it and lay a fuse.'

TEN

BLOODY SUNDOWN

It was the moment of stillness before night. The wind had dropped and the vague reflection of the vanishing sun just showed above a darkening ridge. The mission was silent.

Dusk shrouded the walls, the buildings, the courtyard, and the silent rise in the sand where the powder-box had been buried. Leading from this mound was a thin trail of black powder, imperceptible in the gloom.

'I reckon,' Shane said, 'it won't be long now.'

Father Matthew Lockley was delving into the deep pocket of his cassock, laying out the last of his cartridges on the pew just inside the chapel porch.

'Like me to take a walk to see what they're doing?' Lockley said.

'Nope,' Shane said. 'We stay here, together.'

The priest mopped his bald tonsure. They were crouched just inside the chapel door. Behind them were the dusty pews which stood in rows leading up to the altar and the golden crucifix. In front of them was the courtyard bearing the deadly bomb in its sandy bosom. He let his gaze move to the side of the yard. Sand had been kicked over the trap-door which concealed Jonah and Rebecca.

'Shane,' the priest said, 'you're a hired gunfighter, aren't you?'

Shane grinned. 'Guilty!' he nodded, then added, 'No sermons, please.'

'No sermon,' Father Matthew Lockley assured him. 'I was just figuring that ours is a strange alliance. A hired gunslinger and a priest!'

'An unholy one?'

'Far from it!' The smile on the missioner's face faded and suddenly he was very serious. 'What I was going to say is this. I've had hired guns come here before, men like yourself, Shane. They've stopped here for shelter in storms, and they've all been hellions, Shane. Cruel, dangerous men. But somehow you're different, a lot different. You aren't like them at all.'

146

They heard the distant, muffled drumbeat of hoofs.

A bullet smashed into the front gate, and Shane hastily picked up his rifle.

'Mind, Father,' Shane Preston said, slamming a cartridge into the loading breech, 'come to think of it, you ain't exactly a normal kind of priest!'

Father Lockley's right hand was extended and Shane gripped it firmly. A strange bond had been sealed between two men of different worlds.

The drumbeat of hoofs became louder. Shane pulled the chapel door almost shut and the two men waited as a hail of lead slashed furiously into the gate, rocking it on its hinges. They could hear yelling, the snarl of guns, the occasional screaming whicker of a horse. Still the gate held, but then one hinge snapped and the big door lurched sideways. Eager hands began to rip the shattered gate off the last hinges and it fell away with a splintering crash. Then the iron bar was lifted off the hooks and moments later riders surged liked a tide through the archway.

Standing at the slit, Shane watched as the renegades poured inside.

Most of them were half-breeds, but right behind the main bunch came the Long Knife outfit. At first, the renegades simply wheeled around the edges of the courtyard, guns blazing haphazardly, expecting any instant to encounter the last pocket of resistance. In fact, Kenning himself stood high in his stirrups and yelled to his men, urging them to find the gunfighters and kill them. Three windows in the hall wall were shattered by raking gunfire. One of the chapel's stained glass windows caved in, and the priest groaned. But still no guns roared at the intruders, and bewildered, the raiders began to mill around the center of the yard.

Shane edged the door open a little wider. He whipped out his iron box of vestas. The tiny flare lit up the darkness of the chapel porch as Shane held up the match and prised the door wider. He flicked the flaming match onto the gunpowder trail.

Like a speeding bullet, the flame leaped and scorched along the fuse. Ponies reared, half-breeds screamed in terror as the wild line of fire lit up the night. Pandemonium was breaking loose as the flame seemed to lap at the mound. There was a long moment when time stood still. Then suddenly the bowels of the earth opened and the searing blast rocked every last brick in the mission. Men and horses were blown about like thin sticks in a storm, plastered against the walls, buried in the heaving sand. Renegades collapsed into blackened heaps, two were swallowed up by the widening crater, and one whimpering 'breed wandered stunned and bloodied amidst the swirling smoke. Hardly a man was left on his horse. Dead renegades lay sprawled in the sand, and those who were alive were crawling around like wounded spiders. The big 'breed, Trauba, was trying to claw at his dying horse, and Shane leveled his rifle from the chapel porch. There was a single shot and Trauba slithered into the crater.

Still the smoke rose, a fiery pall in the sundown, and the echoes of the explosion came back in waves from the desert ridges. Gradually they dissipated, and Shane edged out off the porch with his rifle poised.

A bullet ripped past the gunfighter and thudded into the chapel wall, and through the swirling smoke, Shane could see dim figures near the archway. The priest scrambled out to stand alongside him.

'Father,' Shane said. 'When those breeds were blasted to hell, most of the Long Knife outfit were by that arch – and I reckon they ain't so dazed as the rest. Stay here and watch things. I'm taking a look over there.'

The gunfighter ran to the western wall.

Two shots winged overhead, and crouching down in the drifting smoke, Shane saw the three outlaws staked out in the archway. Ryan was edging into view, his face black as charcoal, his shirt ripped. Shane's gun thundered and the outlaw ducked back for cover. The gunfighter flattened himself against the wall as he heard the outlaws grate instructions to each other.

He inched forward. There was the sound of heavy breathing nearby, and whipping around, Shane stared into the naked muzzle of a leveled gun. The gun blast shattered the silence and the half-breed dropped like a rock with Father Lockley's slug in his back.

'Shane!' He heard the whisper from behind him.

He swiveled around to see Jonah Jones crawling up out of the cellar. The old gunfighter's shoulder was dark with blood stains and he stooped awkwardly as he stumbled towards him.

'Rebecca's OK,' Jonah said, wincing. 'But I figured you might need help to clean up these buzzards.'

'Father Lockley's got the 'breeds covered,' Shane said. 'But Kenning's crew is staked out in the archway. Maybe you can keep them occupied for about two minutes. Reckon that's all I need.'

'What are you plannin' to do?' the oldster wheezed.

'Come up from behind them,' Shane told him.

Jonah gaped, but knelt down and trained his rifle on the archway. Two shots rang out in quick succession as Jonah began his covering fire, and Shane backed away in the darkness.

The tall gunhawk slipped back to the chapel. By now the embers had all fled up into the night and even the smoke cloud had been reduced to a few wispy ropes climbing into the night sky. The darkness engulfed Shane Preston as he ran over the broken sands to the foot of the ladder. One bloodied renegade lay sprawled over the lower rungs, and when Shane shoved him aside, he flopped lifelessly down to the ground.

Swiftly, Shane mounted the ladder and stood on the parapet. Raking fire was plastering the walls around the arch, keeping the outlaws low, and when Jonah emptied one gun, he merely tossed it down and drew out his six-gun.

Shane looked over the wall.

The desert was dark, mysterious, the only light a last streak of red in the west. Shane straddled the wall. He knew it was a long drop, but the sand would be soft. Clutching the top of the wall, he levered his lean body over the outside until he was hanging by his fingertips. Then he released his hold and plunged downwards.

He hit the cold sand with a dull thud, sprawling onto his side. The flesh-wound he'd received at Foster's Outpost jarred him when he fell, but Shane shook off the pain and clambered to his feet. He ran softly through the sand to the front corner of the mission and glanced at the outside of the entrance arch. Still Jonah was blasting away at them, and even as Shane edged away from the wall into the desert, he heard the wicked whine of a bullet spinning from the adobe brick. Shane headed into the darkness, circling through the sand until he halted at the edge of the stage trail just beyond the entrance. He could see the backs of the outlaws as they huddled together against the wall. One of Jonah's slugs smashed into the fallen gate, ripping at the outlaws. But then the shooting stopped and Shane figured his pard must be jamming cartridges into his gun. The outlaws slowly edged away from the wall. Hammers of guns were thumbed back. Kenning barked an order.

Shane moved in, his gun leveled.

'Party's over, boys!' the gunfighter rasped in the night. The trio froze.

Kenning's face was shadowed by the night as Shane stepped closer to the archway.

'Put a name to yourself!' Long Knife's voice was still harsh with authority.

'Shane Preston,' the gunfighter said. 'Now if you want to keep on breathing, just stay right where you are and grab sky!'

Slowly, the outlaws raised their hands and stood motionless.

'Jonah!' Shane called out. 'I've got these galoots covered. You can come right on over.'

The oldster shuffled across the yard and halted on

the other side of the arch.

'OK, boys,' Shane said. 'Here's the next move. One by one you'll unbuckle your gun rigs and let them drop – and the first hombre to make a false play gets a bullet in the brain.'

Long Knife's eyes narrowed, 'And after we drop our gun rigs, Preston?'

'We get ready to take you back to the cell in Boulder Bluff,' the gunfighter replied. 'After that? Well, I guess there'll be a fast trial and a faster hanging.'

'Your gun rigs!' Jonah prompted them.

Just then the faint rumble of distant hoofs came to them, and a smile spread over Shane's face.

'Sounds like Donnell's riding in,' he said. 'And a passel of riders with him.'

Cold fear gripped the outlaw trio. Already the rumble was mounting and within a couple of minutes the riders would be here, shattering any last hopes of freedom.

'Don't be loco,' Shane warned them, knowing their desperation. 'We have the drop on you! Just wait here nice and quiet until Donnell rides in. It'll be real interesting when he finds out his neighbor and friend is Long Knife, killer and outlaw!'

The sweat was running into Kenning's eyes. The drumbeat of hoofs was rising to a crescendo.

'Take the bastards!' Kenning screamed like a madman.

Jeb Ryan's hand swooped first for his gun and Jonah's bullet smashed open his head. The outlaw lurched sideways, thudding into Kenning as the bandit leader groped frantically for his own six-gun. Shane let Kenning's hand grasp the gun butt. He waited as the rancher dragged the gun clear from its holster and then squeezed his trigger. There was a deafening roar and the slug burned into Kenning's chest. Without a murmur, Pete Kenning relaxed his grip on the gun. The six-gun slithered down over Kenning's hip and then the outlaw folded into a shapeless heap in the sand beside the bullet-scarred gate.

'How about you?' Shane snapped at Dayman.

But the outlaw's hands were still high. Dayman's fear-filled eyes glanced down at the two men who'd just died and moved to the body of Rodd Lewis who'd been blasted to his doom with most of the 'breeds.

'I'll take my chances with the judge,' Dayman blurted.

Riders surged up the trail, and leaving Jonah to look after Dayman, Shane turned to meet them. Donnell headed the bunch, and as they reined in their foam-flecked horses, he threw himself out of the saddle.

154

'Shane!' Donnell's voice was an agonized croak. 'Rebecca – where is she? How is she?'

'Alive, Mr Donnell,' Shane said. 'Stopped a slug, but she'll be OK. If you get one of your boys to look after this owlhoot here, Jonah will take you to her.'

'Thank God!' Donnell said fervently.

'And, Mr Donnell,' Shane said, 'I'll be seeing you in a couple of minutes.'

'Meaning?'

'There's a little chore I have to attend to,' the gun-fighter said.

Donnell frowned as Shane Preston strode away from the mission into the night.

Shane didn't look over his shoulder but he knew that as of now Donnell would be hurrying to a reunion with his daughter, his ranch hands would be rounding up any of Trauba's men who were still alive. He'd leave them to take care of things at the fort, because he knew that there was one last duty he had to perform. The sand was soft and cold beneath him. He walked past the crumpled body of a half-breed beside his pinto pony and side-stepped another bloodied corpse. The wind was rising and when he reached the crest it whipped up the dust around his boots. He stood still, just listening.

For a long time he could hear only the low, steady moan of the wind.

Momentarily, the wind seemed to drop, and the other sound came to him. It was hardly a human sound. It was some unearthly groan, primitive and faint, and Shane strode quickly in the direction it came from.

He felt the sagebrush lash his levis as he waded through the dark bed. He heard the groan again, coming from somewhere to his left. Shane turned his head and walked slowly towards the dark shape.

The gunfighter halted, staring ahead at the spread-eagled figure roped over the mound. Four stakes had been hammered into the sand and the hands and feet of Oliver Stobie were lashed to them. Shane went closer and stood over the body. Stobie was naked, but the gunfighter could hardly see an inch of flesh on him. The fiendish ants covered him in a brown, moving blanket. Hardened gunslinger as he was, Shane wanted to turn his face away from the ghastly scene of man's cruelty and nature's revenge for disturbing the ants' nest.

Shane crouched down beside the quivering remains of the man Rebecca had been going to marry. 'Stobie!' he whispered.

The ant-filled mouth opened but only a groan escaped.

Shane whipped out his knife and sliced through the rawhide lashing Stobie's limbs to the stakes. The dandy didn't even have the strength to roll off the anthill. He merely lay there, a wretched, dying man whose flesh had almost been stripped from his bones.

With a supreme effort, Oliver Stobie forced a broken plea from his lips.

'Kill – me! For – God's sake – kill me, Preston!'

Shane swallowed. If Stobie had been an animal, he'd have blasted him into oblivion right away. But Oliver Stobie was a human being.

'Please! I'm begging you!'

Shane took one of the spare guns he'd used from his belt. He weighed it in the palm of his hand.

'Some folks would say you're all-yeller,' Shane said, bending over Stobie. 'Reckon I'm gonna give you the chance to show yourself that you've got some guts after all.'

He placed the gun in Stobie's hollowed left hand.

He stood up and walked away into the night. The chill wind moaned around him as he began the lonely trek back to the mission. He reached the crest and a sharp, muffled gun blast rang out in the night. Oliver Stobie had found an ounce of courage in his last, darkest hour.

Father Matthew Lockley had discarded his powder-burned black cassock for the purple one he wore to mass. There was a golden crucifix hanging around his neck, and standing beside the lean-to stable where Shane was saddling his horse, Lockley looked like he was about to conduct worship.

'There's something I want you to know, Father,' Shane said as he tightened his saddle-cinch. 'I've just had a word with Ridge Donnell. In a couple of minutes he wants to be shown around the mission.'

'Shown around!' the missioner gasped. 'Holy Mother! What will he see? Broken windows, smashed pews, bullet-scarred walls! I can't show him those things!'

'Those things are precisely what he wants to see,' Shane said.

'Huh?'

'You see, Father,' Shane explained, 'Donnell's not exactly a pauper, and he's so happy to get his daughter back he's in the mood to be real generous. In fact, he wants you to estimate the cost of putting Apache Wells Mission back into shape.'

A broad smile lit up the priest's face.

'Furthermore,' Shane said, 'he says he'll make a donation to your funds so you can plan for extensions later on.'

An even broader smile now illuminated Father Lockley's face.

'Reckon you'd better go and catch up with him while he's in a spendin' mood!'

The little priest shook Shane's hand warmly. 'I'll be seeing you again?' he asked.

Shane grinned. 'When we're next passing by, we'll drop into the mission and come to church.'

'Miracles never cease!' the priest said fervently.

'Fact is,' Shane said wryly, 'I'm kinda interested in hearing the sorta sermon a gun-totin' priest preaches.'

Minutes later Shane and Jonah were riding across the yard. A crisp check for one thousand dollars reposed in Shane's pocket, and Donnell was walking around with the priest, waiting to write another.

They headed through the archway.

'Shane!'

She was in the shadows just beyond the arch.

'Reckon I'll ride on ahead,' Jonah Jones grinned.

Shane reined in and Rebecca Donnell looked up at him. They waited until the oldster was swallowed up by the night.

'I want to thank you,' she said. 'For everything, Shane.' He remained in the saddle.

'Not only for the rescue,' she said softly. 'But for the way you helped me feel decent again. Shane, I – I had a word to my father.'

'Oh?'

'Shane, he needs a good ramrod. He pays real well – ask any man who works for him. You could have the

159

job, and we'd find a job for Jonah, too. Besides, I'd like to have you around for other reasons.'

He saw the frank promise her eyes held for him, and a thousand other men would have jumped down from their horses to claim that promise. But not so Shane Preston. He switched his eyes from her and looked out at the darkness of the wasteland. There could be no rest, no woman for Shane Preston until he tracked down and killed his wife's murderer. Until then, he'd hire out his gun to protect the innocent and to earn the money which let him keep riding the lonely trails. Right now those trails were beckoning him, and he had to obey their call because somewhere out there Scarface was living and breathing, and some day there would be the last showdown.

Shane bent over and kissed her cheek. 'So long, Rebecca,' he said.

Her eyes were misty. 'You'll be back some day, won't you?'

'Maybe, Rebecca.'

He urged Snowfire away from the archway and headed up to the crest where Jonah Jones was waiting for him.

Together, they rode out.